MW00787701

BIRTH
of the
BLACK
ORCHIDS

A BLACK ORCHID ENTERPRISES MYSTERY

M. R. DIMOND

Copyright © 2021 by M. R. Dimond

All rights reserved.

No part of this book may be reproduced in any form or by any electronic or mechanical means, including information storage and retrieval systems, without written permission from the author, except for the use of brief quotations in a book review.

Published in the United States by Rock Rose Press.

BIRTH

of the

BLACK

ORCHIDS

PART I
BIRTH OF THE BLACK ORCHIDS

A LIGHT-HEARTED CHRISTMAS TALE OF GOING
HOME, STARTING OVER, AND MURDER
—WITH CATS

NEW BEGINNINGS

It was a perfect day to drive the Jag until the road ran out. Hurricane season had made its shame-faced exit, and the three cold days of Central Texas winter were still in the future, typical for the third week of December. In five hours I could be cruising with the top down along the Gulf of Mexico, tasting the salty breeze, just being myself, not JD Thompson, Attorney at Law or any other suffix, carefree as long as I didn't think about the eternal loan payments.

That wasn't going to happen, one reason being that you have to show up for your own office's grand opening, like you have show up for your own wedding, or so I've been told. So here I stood in Christmas apparel (negotiated down to a green dress shirt and red tie), my feet planted as though braced for an attack, in front of a massive red brick Victorian mansion. Two turrets bulged out on either side of the house like guard stations. Downstairs they held offices, and upstairs, bedrooms. They gave me a sense of doom that I couldn't explain—I didn't even know about the murder yet. Maybe it was the thought of trying to scrape up rent and bills from legal clients in a town with a population of 7,200. But having cast that die, I lined up with my two partners behind our new bronze sign, which listed the name of our firm, the principals, and our specialties.

Another line assured people that both Spanish and Vietnamese were spoken here. Many Beauchamp (pronounced Beecham) residents might use the first, but the last person to need the second, Johnny's grandfather, died several years ago. Johnny wanted to include "detective," but Dianne suggested that we consider the sign's cost and advertise only the embryonic businesses, not the imaginary ones.

Not that Johnny's an imaginary detective. In sophomore year, Dianne collected her friends and rented a ramshackle house, thereafter known as Casa Cortez, just off campus. She included Johnny and me for the illusion of safety. I can loom threateningly, and Johnny has a black belt in martial arts. He also notices more than most people, and soon he was the specialist in finding lost objects, a constant problem in a house of ten or so residents and their constant stream of friends and lovers. When his reputation spread, the neighborhood turned to him to find lost objects, pets, and children. I think he lowered the crime rate of the area just with his constant questions and searches—criminals learned to practice their craft a few blocks over, beyond the range of Sherlock of Becker Street. He expanded his skills to finding evidence in the kind of accusations that plague college students and even solved a murder, something no one wants to repeat, except maybe him. But he doesn't have an investigator's license, and that matters to Dianne. She's also the one that said we needed an umbrella organization for our three divergent specialties. She knows these things. Mostly we take her word.

Chantal Gaumont, friend, party planner, music director, and photographer, called me back to the present as she positioned her phone on a tripod and yelled, "JD, bring the Jag to the front parking lot. I'll do a wide shot and get it in too."

"I sold it," I said.

They turned to me with the gaping expressions of day-old dead fish. I guess this was the most shocking thing I'd said in ten years.

"But your father gave you the Jaguar when you passed the bar," exclaimed Johnny, as though I'd violated some law of physics.

I bit back words I wouldn't want my grandmother to read. "Correction: He made a down payment. I didn't think I could make the payments after leaving a corporate law firm for private practice." That fear also kept me at my old job in Austin until yesterday. I wanted to grab every last billable hour from Ye Old Firm of Dewey, Cheatem, and Howe. (I don't want to spread their names around. They're lawyers, after all). I moved into Gregg House just last night, weeks after the others. I couldn't have come earlier if I wanted to, with everyone texting me daily to run around Austin in search of absolute essentials for this party: esoteric cooking ingredients, more Christmas decorations and greenery, delicacies to join the spread of food Johnny was creating to feed a small country, even a black orchid plant.

"It was such fun to ride in the Jag," mourned Dianne, who insists that she has a mind above money. How is that even possible for an accountant?

"Eating's even more fun," I said, not bothering to describe the weightless feeling as thousands of dollars of debt vanished. Now for the student loans!

Chantal shrugged. Chipper as those Mentos commercials from childhood, she ties knots and moves on. "Well, go get what you're driving now."

I folded my arms over my chest. "Hyundai Sonata. Couple years old, in my favorite color: paid for!" To all the pop-eyed stares, I said,

"There's not many cars that someone six-foot-three can get into without getting a concussion."

"I wouldn't know," Chantal muttered, being five-foot-nothing on tiptoe. "Never mind. Stand behind your name on the sign and—" She yelled an improbable obscenity. Dianne and I burst into snorts of laughter, and even Johnny smiled naturally, once he'd analyzed her words and defined them as a joke.

Having reduced us to our natural selves instead of Young Professionals with pokers applied up our anatomies, Chantal snapped away, each click a muffled gunshot, right through the heart of my career.

Sure, lawyers can leave Corporate World and open their own office. There's lots of advice on how to do that, but none of it mentions partnering with your college housemates and bandmates, including your three-time ex and a veterinarian who, after earning BS and DVM degrees, crashed out of zoo vet school, into the psych ward, and then into an ashram. Nor does this advice include setting up in the middle of both nowhere and Texas.

As a white Lexus pulled into the front parking lot, Chantal did a yoga twist to get us and the car into the frame. We were in fact connected to the Lexus. Johnny's parents, aunt, and uncle poured out of it. Somewhere there was a sister, but she wasn't in the car. I think I met her once at Johnny's first graduation.

The Ly family went into synchronized elder assistance. I gave them a 10 for the smooth flip of the walker from the trunk and its expert unfolding, not to mention their grace in sliding it into Grandmother Ly's hands as they handed her out of the back seat.

Their tense smiles as they marched toward us barely masked their worried hope that Johnny would be okay, that his new cat clinic would be exactly the new start he needed. I felt my own facial muscles mirroring their anxiety. A glance at Dianne showed the same.

Johnny's grandmother started the Christmas open house tradition in self-defense when she moved into Gregg House over fifty years ago. She'd just returned from her stint as a nurse in the Vietnam war, accompanied by her new Vietnamese husband and baby, Johnny's father. She discovered that everyone in Beauchamp wanted to see the interior of the town's old mansion.

Now that she was retiring to an assisted living community in nearby Austin, it seemed like a good business strategy to introduce our new firm when the whole town would show up. Maybe they would remember us when they needed a lawyer, accountant, cat vet, possibly a detective, or even an ABBA tribute band. We keep trying to retire the band, but we keep getting gigs, thanks to the constant marketing efforts of both Chantal and Dianne's event-planning mother. Maybe that's a good thing now.

The Lys' open house was a top holiday event in Beauchamp, right up there with the live Nativity at the Catholic church, where one time the friendly beasts went off-script and into a full-scale rumble. Donkeys are like that. Now the role of the donkey is played by someone's old white pony wearing the equine equivalent of Spock ears, which caused the event to lose points.

We didn't know it then, but our open house would take the all-time prize.

"Johnny, let's get a shot of you and your family." Chantal jerked her head to call Dianne and me close to her. In the time it took his grandmother to clump over to the sign and the Lys to properly align, Chantal whispered, "Guys, how's Johnny going to get through this all-afternoon bash? He never stayed longer than a half hour at any of our parties."

"That's all he ever agreed to. Half an hour for parties and one social event each month, like a movie or dancing," added Dianne, a slight worry line etched in her forehead. "He can take breaks today, maybe hide in his grandfather's meditation building."

Gregg House's acre-plus surroundings included a jumble of buildings behind the house. I'd seen only the octagonal meditation room and a barn on its way to becoming a cat habitat. Mrs. Ly's renovations and improvements having fallen behind schedule, the Texas brush, always ready to devour any sliver of civilization, still covered most of the acre, inhibiting my exploration.

"I don't know," I said.

"For sure," said Chantal as she focused her camera.

I'm still amazed all the things Chantal does to support her one true desire to sing. Because her family, with vivid memories of their resettlement after Hurricane Katrina, wanted her to be able to make a living, she picked a college major from the beginning of the alphabet and then spent most of her time in the music school. She met Dianne in Accounting 101 and was a first and constant presence at Casa Cortez.

Chantal survives by singing, doing taxes, and scraping other side gigs. A diabetic, she copes with parties by throwing them and shoving the food and drink she can't have into everybody else. We hired her to put on our open house in our constant effort to shove money in her direction. She doesn't *want* to live here, because Beauchamp has no music scene, but she has taken over the fourth bedroom upstairs.

We've got history, me and my friends. I pulled out an old, old, almost origin story. "Thing is, Johnny was sixteen when he started college."

"And he was assigned as your roommate in the dorm, and you took care of him like a little brother. We know," said Dianne, waving at the motorcade pulling up, full of her relatives arriving early for photos and the special families-only tour, an hour before the official starting time.

"The usual jerks asked if he was having his birthday party at Chuck E. Cheese. Johnny said he never had that kind of party as a kid, and it would be fantastic to do it now. He invited all the guys in the dorm and his classes. He arranged it like a kid's party, but on a weeknight when the place was deserted. The management even let us in the ball pit when the kids were gone. Johnny had a great time, and it was one of the best parties I've ever been to."

"Oh yeah?" asked the official party planner, frosty as the sherbet she dumped in the punch bowl before this photo shoot.

I hurried on. "So he might be okay if it's his own party."

"Maybe," agreed Dianne, doubt heavy in her voice. "But we don't have a ball pit."

"Hunh," said Chantal, closing the conversation. She waved the Ly family away and the newcomers toward the sign. "Dianne, get your family lined up. I'll have to go pano to get them all in the shot."

Dianne's family lives a good four-hour drive away. Her siblings and cousins who arrived the night before to serve as Chantal's minions poured out of the house to greet the new arrivals: her parents, grand-parents, aunts, uncles, and younger cousins, all piling out of their cars now, unable to resist a chance to support Dianne. If Dianne needed chemo and round-the-clock care, they would have rallied around her, but attending her party was better.

Dianne's mother, in the lead as always, gasped when she got close enough to read the sign. Breaking off the intended embrace, she lifted tragic eyes to her eldest daughter's face. "'G. Dianne.' Lupita, could you not even spell out the name I gave you to honor the Blessed Virgin?"

"The sign company charged by the letter," said Dianne, tossing the section of her long, gleaming locks that wasn't captured in an updo. She didn't point out that *Lupita* is a nickname for *Guadalupe*.

Just as a statement of fact, Dianne is the most beautiful woman in the world. She first burst into my sight at our University of Texas freshman mixer. I must have set a record in the cross-gym sprint. I spit out some words about doing something with her sometime, and she, already with that faint bored expression beautiful women develop, asked, "*¿Hablas español?*"

"*Sí, desde la niñez,*" I replied. I didn't need her amused expression to tell me how I sounded, so I rushed on to say (in Spanish) that my mother thought it was so important to speak Spanish in Texas that she hired a nanny—okay, housecleaner—to teach me.

Dianne conceded and switched to English. "I am very fond of Latin dancing."

"Me too," I said.

"Your mother thought that important too?" Her cathedral-arched eyebrows indicated disbelief.

"She did," I said, instantly grateful for all the Saturday morning ballroom classes I'd grumbled about. "All ballroom dances." I held out my hand as my guardian angel put on a Gloria Estefan tune.

And that's how you get a date with Dianne: (1) Speak Spanish and (2) Dance.

Ten years on, the years are still kind to her, downright generous, and today she rocked a splendid flared dress of emerald-green velour. Touches of scarlet glistened in sequined fascinators in her shiny dark hair down to her be-blinged ballerina flats. Add her mother, sisters, aunts, and cousins to the scene, and the total effect overwhelmed the senses, especially when combined with the gardenia perfume the Cortez women love. My head swam as I inhaled its aromatic scent, just on the edge of too sweet.

Chantal wheedled them into remaining frozen for photos before she switched to video as, young and old, they all chattered, so excited, because opening your own business was a thing to celebrate.

"I bet you can use these videos on TikTok," said Chantal, pleased with herself. "And the photos are going to be great. The light's perfect. Who's doing your social media?"

"JD," replied both Dianne and Johnny, almost to the porch, behind his family.

Which is how it goes. Johnny and Dianne do their specialties, Chantal does all her stuff, and I do whatever's left. Maybe Chantal would help with the social media, at least show me how.

"Where are your people, JD?" asked Chantal as the Cortez family thundered towards the behemoth house that was going to change my life.

"Maybe they misunderstood the time for the Families Only Tour," I said, casual to the max. I told them the wrong time, so as not to have to hear their opinions of JD's latest stunt, which couldn't be good. "Let's not wait for them."

GREGG HOUSE

I had three goals for the day: to charm or at least not to repulse Beauchamp; to shore up Johnny through this event, which promised to be the biggest one I'd ever see him attend other than college graduation; and to avoid Dianne's mother's matchmaking schemes. No one grieved more than Conchita Cortez when Dianne and I broke up, every time.

To achieve the third aim, I lagged well behind the others and pretended to look at the scenery from the front porch. We first saw Gregg House in the early fall, a cheery, colorful time of year in Texas. In those days, the cotton-candy crepe myrtles fluffed around the house in shades of pinks, the Day-of-the-Dead marigolds along the walkways blazed orange and yellow, and the esperanza bushes along the fence hung heavy with their yellow bells. Now the crepe myrtles were stripped bare, the marigolds were compost, and the esperanza bushes had dropped both bells and leaves. *Esperanza* means "hope," now gone for the year.

Once I crossed the threshold, the house grabbed my attention again. I caught my breath at the vaulted, frescoed ceilings in a gallery the length of a sportsball floor that extended to the back door, the open floor plan before open floor plans were cool—way before, having been built in 1897. I was surprised the Catholics weren't genuflecting. To the eyes of a generic Protestant (no traditions and proud of it!), Gregg House looked like a cathedral. The bristling greenery of the Christmas decor, including a spangled Christmas tree the size of a middle-aged redwood, added to the majesty.

The acoustics were awesome. I tested them last night with the baby grand piano at the far end of the gallery hall, across from the shiny, newly renovated kitchen (because nobody wants history in their kitchen). After years of wearing headphones and pounding on an electric keyboard, it felt great to have music roiling around me. My roommates put up with it for a while because I claimed to be practicing for today. Now people were roaming the gallery, but I could hear distinct parts of conversations from the front of house instead of a mush of voices, from admiring comments on the black orchids I brought from Austin, which made me wince, to exclamations over the kitchen and the piano at the back of the house.

As I waited while Dianne handed her mother one of her Latina cards—"Guadalupe Dianne Cortez y Jáquez, CPA, CFE," in a speck-sized font—I glanced behind me at each of the turret offices: Dianne's shimmering in sleek glass and delicate chrome, with a silvery nameplate by the door announcing "G. D. Cortez" in dainty script. On the opposite side, my office proclaimed the majesty of the law with heavy antiques from Johnny's grandmother's grandparents. By the door someone had slapped a Post-it note with "JD Thompson" scribbled in a fat-bladed Sharpie. I snatched it and crumpled it in my pocket. People would have to guess. Post-its didn't go with the decor.

We barricaded our offices and the bedrooms with baby gates draped in red velour and holly sprigs. Mrs. Ly developed them long ago to keep the marauding hordes out of private spaces. Dianne expressed gratitude that people couldn't paw through her underwear. I worried more about the office equipment.

While the crowd made disorganized progress down the hall, I pretended to study the reception desk. My gaze bounced away from the three-bloomed black orchid plant to the artful display of cards and coupons scattered around the guest book. At first I saw only Chantal's cards for all her skills. I thought she didn't want to live here full time. I spotted some cards for our band as well (Multi-ABBA, originally Multicultural ABBA, which no one could say or spell, but a good description of a group ranging from lily white to Mississippi River brown). Then I found those for the current enterprise: Free well-pet exam! Free basic tax return! Free twenty-minute legal consultation!— wait, what? I should have moved in earlier, to foil or hear about these plans, even if it meant chopping ingredients for Johnny, applying sequins to all nonsentient surfaces for Chantal, and doing any scut-work that occurred to Dianne. It occurred to me that I was now signed up for unlimited years of "JD can do it."

I didn't mind running all over Austin for weeks in pursuit of every-thing the others thought vital to this day. I could endure playing piano for Chantal's carol singing and admit with good grace to having been in a band. In Texas nobody trusts anybody who was never in a band.

My gaze bounced away from the desk surface to the photos mounted on the left wall. I groaned at the first one: a Multi-ABBA publicity photo. Admitting I was in a band was one thing; a photo of my younger self prancing about in a yellow satin suit would not inspire confidence in potential clients.

The flashy yellow satin (lovingly stitched by Chantal and Dianne, with me contributing the parts that any idiot could do) did go nicely with the heavy gold and red velvet furniture from the 1940s. The somber chairs and sofa faced a handsome Vietnamese silk painting, also gold and red, on the opposite wall (and over the Lys' big screen TV). Above the chairs and sofa, our own mementos replaced many of the Ly family photos: graduations, Dianne's *quinceañera* and dance performances (bal-let, *folklórico*, Latin ballroom), and—Ack! Even a photo of Dianne and me at the University of Texas' yearly Great Waltz. At least I was in a tux, not yellow satin. As I stepped forward to figure out what year it was, I caught the gimlet eye of Johnny's grandmother, sunk into a throne-like red velvet chair. She reminded me of the piano teacher who knew at a glance that I hadn't practiced. I suppressed the impulse to run and the unreasonable anger that everything was her fault, although it was.

She was the one who found Johnny at the ashram, caring for the resident feral cat colony, and asked whether he wanted to return to zoo vet school—he had at least a year left—or if not, did he want to take over her historic mansion in Beauchamp. She would remodel the house one last time to include a vet clinic. Like a be-gentled movie villain, he held and stroked the last kittens (because he'd neutered and spayed the tribe) as he said that any more school would be bad for his health. Maybe he could limp by with his bachelor's in biology, regular vet school, and veterinary acupuncture training. He'd prefer to have a cat clinic, though of course he'd help any suffering animal.

When he invited old college housemates to join him in Beauchamp, Dianne and I fell over ourselves accepting. Dianne's vast, prestigious accounting firm was sucking out her soul like Ye Old Firm was doing to me, and neither of us could believe we'd taken out many-digit loans to earn multiple degrees for this extraordinary rendition.

After that first giddy flush, like any new relationship, a lump settled into my gut that felt like the size and weight of those cannon-balls at the Alamo. Every day I made a list of advantages and disadvan-tages for staying where I was and flying free, as I persisted in thinking of it. Except for that one time I was called as a public defender, the only advantages of Ye Old Firm were its salary, prestige, and health insurance. Those were more important to me than they used to be, but they couldn't outweigh the prospect of escaping law in box, a box of an apartment, and a ever-shrinking box of friendships as my work hours lengthened and focused on the corporate law world. All these boxes had enough room to turn around if I hunched my shoulders inward.

I was sure that the tiny matriarch's piercing eyes could see my turmoil, but all she asked was, "Are you settled in well?"

"Nice, very nice," I stammered. "Beautiful place. Love the office."

Dianne tells me I can go on like that forever. Fortunately she called from further down the hall. "JD, *Mami* says the downstairs bathroom still smells like bleach. If you're not coming on the tour, you can wipe it down again."

I sighed as she explained this tragedy in five acts, that the contractors broke a bottle of bleach in the bathroom. I heard about it for a week, everything they'd tried and everyone they consulted. I'd already taken one turn at scrubbing, and I'd been in the house less than twenty-four hours. They kept the window open for days, not a hardship in a Central Texas December.

After an apologetic smile to Mrs. Ly, I fled to the bathroom, also lovingly decorated like the rest of the house. The speckled faux finish evoked Tuscany, or maybe an Olive Garden restaurant, though I don't know why anyone wants Italy in the bathroom. At least the lavender-herbal-citrus smells from cleansers and scent-disguisers had faded, unlike the bleach. Telling myself this was the wonderful world of having your own office, I sponged a liberal amount of water across the walls and floor. Even with the door wide open, I felt dizzy. And depressed, because somewhere on Dianne's laptop was an embryonic spreadsheet for household chores, like those she made for Casa Cortez. In ten years I should have made progress instead of circling back to Start.

She was still soothing her mother, but on another topic. "Yes, *Mamí*, we ordered something from every restaurant and food truck in town, and I made a spreadsheet so that we don't favor one place over another."

Dianne thinks the world and probably your soul can be saved by spreadsheets. Don't get her started on the 3D equivalents. As an event planner, her mother agrees.

The chattering families grew fainter as they poured through the back door to look at the acre of land and buildings behind the house. Someone in heavy boots tromped in from the back door.

"I came to pick up the last check for the remodeling, Mrs. Ly."

Mrs. Ly's gravelly voice carried to my location. "Hello, Matt. I hoped you'd be by sooner to go over the punch list. If you can't get through it before the open house, you can come back tomorrow and finish."

"Mrs. Ly, I'm leaving today and don't know when or if I'll be back. I just can't go on here since my partner died. Chris Herald, you know. We'd worked together since high school." The silence afterwards didn't convey sympathy. He continued, "I'm going back to the old homestead in Mexico. My grandfather's getting up in years. He says he can get me work. I really need that money."

"Your partner's death is very sad," said Mrs. Ly in trenchant tones. "But I don't know what it has to do with these defects and shoddy workmanship. Chris was always very careful, but after he died, someone tried to fix the remaining issues with a caulk gun. You can start by helping JD get the bleach smell out of the bathroom."

After a few stomps—the cherrywood floor magnified even light steps—a man in his mid-thirties stood at the bathroom door. He might have been younger, but Central Texas dries and fries outdoor workers to a husk. White skin blisters and blond hair bleaches into straw.

He stuck out a hand that felt like an attack. "Matt Davies. I'm in charge of the remodeling work."

I rinsed and dried my hands to shake his. "JD Thompson. I hope you know what to do about the smell." I described all the attempts I could remember.

"Sorry about that. One of the guys broke a bottle of bleach when he was trying to clean up our mess. Nobody realized it, and it leaked out overnight and soaked everything." He scowled, deep in thought. "Baking soda?"

So we scrubbed with baking soda and brought in a small fan to blow at high speed with the window open. It would have to do.

Matt pulled the punch list from his pocket and waved it like a royal decree. "Her Highness wants all this nit-picky stuff done before she gives me my last check. You want to show me what she's talking about?"

I shrugged. "I would if I could, but I wasn't here when she and her grandson followed the inspector around."

Matt's eyes bulged. "Inspector? She didn't need to hire an inspector."

"I understand she always does when she has work done on the house."

The families returned from the outdoor tour with shoes clattering and much laughing. As they headed for the stairs, I called to Johnny, who brandished his own copy of the punch list as he joined us. I doubted Matt would get much sympathy from him either.

"Let's start with the clinic," Johnny suggested. "You can come back tomorrow for the kitchen. I don't want to mix construction materials with the food."

"But I'm leaving later today for Mexico, to see my grandfather," Matt protested.

Dianne took a detour to lean over Johnny and sniff the bathroom air. Her nose twitched and I raised my hands, helpless. She sighed and followed the others up the stairs. "Like that gringo has a Mexican grandfather," she muttered in Spanish.

I understood, but Matt either didn't or didn't hear her. He followed Johnny out of the bathroom and said, "Let's at least look at the kitchen. Maybe I can fix it without chemicals."

"Don't get out the caulk gun," said Johnny. "I'm still baking."

I grinned as they made their way toward the kitchen, past the Christmas tree and the food tables awash with treats. Matt wouldn't make his flight that day. As long as I've known him, Johnny's said, "As my sainted-if-she-weren't-Jewish grandmother says, 'There's kindness, and then there's being a fool.'"

"What's this 'Specialty Diet' table?" Matt asked as they passed the first food table, the one opposite the Christmas tree by the staircase.

I shook my head. He'd be sorry he asked.

"I try to make sure there's something for everyone," Johnny enthused. "So we have kosher, vegetarian, vegan (nondairy), low sodium, no nuts, low carb, low or no sugar." His voice sorrowful, he confessed, "JD bought the no-nuts food from a bakery in Austin. I can't guarantee that my prep area is nut free. We had an allergic roommate in college, and we were very careful for her sake. But I've cooked for diabetics for ten years, and I'm confident that what I've put out is low carb." Chantal kissed his cheek in thanks as she walked by with more trays. Johnny jumped and so did his voice. "Of course, not all diabetics eat low carb, so I have other things too."

Smiling at Johnny being Johnny, I strolled to the staircase to greet the descending family troops, Dianne in the lead. Looking like St. Somebody on her way to martyrdom, she took my hand, and whispered, "You said you'd help me with this."

"Yeah, but do you think now—"

"Excuse me, everyone. Excuse me." Dianne said in her *Hermana Mayor* voice, the eldest sister who commanded respect—or else. As they quieted, she drew a deep breath. "I have something—JD and I have something to say." She looked at me for courage.

I assumed my courtroom demeanor, serious as the graveyard or accounts payable.

Her parents exchanged trembling smiles and squeezed hands. Mr. Cortez looked from his wife to Dianne with proud happiness. I quailed. I like them both. The sisters and cousins murmured in high-pitched, musical whispers.

Chantal, on the other hand, looked like she'd seen an unfriendly ghost. Johnny looked puzzled as he searched our faces for clues.

Dianne continued, "Some of you were giggling over the sleeping arrangements—I saw you, Tima and Candy—and I want you to know that what you saw is the truth. Johnny, JD, and I have separate bedrooms; Chantal too, when she's here. JD and I are not living together, not that way, or getting married. We're just roommates, like we've been for most of the last ten years."

Mrs. Cortez burst into tears. Her husband glared at Dianne. The aunts scolded and lobbed angry looks our way. The cousins and sisters giggled, happy for the drama, glad they hadn't caused it.

"What did I say?" whispered Dianne, terrified, shrinking against me.

"You were perfect, *querida*," I said, pronouncing it as badly as I always do as I squeezed her shoulders and choked back laughter.

Johnny edged toward us and whispered through the harangues, "I'm not the social interaction expert, but my guess is that her family expected a different announcement."

"Bingo," I breathed out, hoping Dianne wouldn't hear. "But we all know Dianne's better with numbers than with people."

Johnny looked amazed that other people might make social gaffes.

Chantal clapped her hands and commanded, "All right, elves, we gotta get pumped. JD?" She nudged me to the baby grand piano and whispered a song and a key.

I pounded out something about something going on and on—hey, I never sing melody. Dianne harmonized with Chantal and started a sixteen-bar line dance she choreographed in the distant past. Soon her sisters Lourdes, Tima, and Candy; brother Zap; and older cousins joined in, leaving only the elementary school cousins looking on, stars in their eyes. The littlest one, age seven, finally led them into the dance. The embroidered butterflies in her hair and on her bright green dress quivered. Of course her name was Mariposa: Butterfly.

Golden glitters joining the shiny dark tresses told me my family had arrived, at least my twin sisters, Merry and Cherry. A few bars later, I caught sight of my father and grandfather, Attorney Jay Thompson and former US Attorney Jim Thompson, and my grand-mother. The attorneys looked as sour as last year's pickles, and my grandmother, my first music teacher, looked delighted. Grandmother is fragile these days, but she made a beeline through the dancers to sit beside me on the piano bench.

Chantal clapped again, stopping the music and dancing on the instant. "Ten minutes until curtain," she boomed. "Food elves, meet me in the kitchen. Tour guides, meet with Zap at the stairs. Santa's elves, meet with Lourdes by the Christmas tree. Principals, to the door. People are looking inside already."

Dianne retrieved a battered pink camera from a kitchen drawer and held it up. "Please take photos when you can—and get people's permission for JD to publish them on social media, with or without names. I set up a digital signing document on Google Drive. You can send your photos to our cloud account. Does anyone need a camera?"

The elves all snickered and held up their latest-greatest phones. Little Mariposa pushed through the crowd and called, "I can take pictures, Lupita."

Dianne smiled as she handed over the camera, her great-grand-mother's gift for Dianne's high school graduation from Santa María Guadalupe Catholic College Prep. (Go, Fighting Handmaids!) With her last paycheck from Accountants R Us, Dianne upgraded her phone to the stratosphere, but she'll keep her *bisabuela*'s gift forever. She stooped down to show her little cousin how to work it, necessary because only dinosaurs own actual cameras now.

I relinquished the piano bench to Grandmother, who rippled through dreamy Christmas tunes as I joined Johnny and Dianne. We almost crashed into the food elves, pouring from the kitchen with plates of everything, trying to find space for it on the already full tables.

"That table by the stairs doesn't have much on it," said a Cortez cousin. "We could put the overflow there."

Johnny whipped around like he'd been slapped. "Do not put other food on the special diets table. Everything is properly labeled so that people can tell what's in them."

"That's right," agreed Chantal. "It would be a bad thing if a diabetic got the wrong food."

"But you said the guests will bring food too. What if they say it's hypoallergenic or something?" asked my sister Cherry, all aglow in, of course, Christmas red. Having known Johnny since they were nine, my sisters have as much respect for him as they do for their brother—less than the average August rainfall in Texas.

As Johnny's expression turned stony, I cut in. "How about the elves put a card on the donated treat and add 'allegedly' to the description, like 'wheat-free-dairy-free-sugar-free, egg-free *allegedly.*' Then people will know there's a doubt."

Johnny looked relieved. "That would be acceptable, at least temporarily, until I can talk to the person and examine what they brought. Come get me when that happens."

Dianne and I each grabbed one of his arms and bulldozed him to the front door. I faked an apologetic shrug as we passed my grim-faced father and grandfather, who were not feeling the holiday spirit.

ARRIVALS

*I*t started great. Rosemary, Jia, and Shanice, former denizens of Casa Cortez, our college group house/insane asylum, fell through the front door into our open arms with joyous squealing.

"Rosemary," said Johnny into the hair (or extension) over her ear, "Come see the special diets table! I thought about you while putting it together."

Dianne and I shared an eye roll over Jia's and Shanice's heads. Chantal taught us about diabetes; Rosemary, peanut allergies. We learned what to do for them in emergencies. We never had to call an ambulance, but Johnny still held monthly emergency care drills as long as they were in the house.

Jia and Shanice each waved a diamond-encrusted ring finger and exchanged sugary looks. Dianne and I hugged them harder with more congratulations. They followed Rosemary and Johnny down the hall, where more squeals erupted as Chantal discovered them. "And we're going to sing for you, and make your cake, and your dinners, maybe even your dresses, if you want." Dianne's eyes widened; she'd be on the hook for several of those tasks. Me, I'd just be involved with the music, unless Dianne and Chantal called all hands on deck for bejeweling the dresses.

Johnny, looking pleased at Rosemary's praise, returned just in time to greet another guest we knew. Mrs. Leigh Brandon was an oil baron's widow, as elegant as money could make her. She lived across the street in a neat pastel blue house that not only had all its parts (unlike many Beauchamp residences), but had them maintained and scrubbed to a glow. She was accompanied by her two middle-aged daughters, Claire and Melanie, and more grandchildren than I could count in the time it took to introduce ourselves.

Miss Leigh, as we say in the South, placed a decorative box in Johnny's hands and stage-whispered so that no one beyond three blocks away could hear, "Johnny, I've brought you some of Claire's holiday-decorated treats for today, and I have some bigger boxes for you at home."

Claire owned a cannabis bakery in Colorado, where such things are legal. Bringing it across state lines, not so much. Her mother swore by Claire's chocolates as a cure for "nerves," as we also say in the South. Last weekend she brought Johnny a box after hearing from his grand-mother that he was nervous.

That's one way to describe his never-ending fast and furious educa-tional journey. Johnny always did school brilliantly, right up to when he couldn't anymore.

I don't know if he finished off the previous enhanced chocolates—I try to maintain plausible deniability, being an officer of the court—but he smiled his thanks as he accepted the new box. As he left to, I hoped, hide it, Dianne beamed the respectful smile she reserves for elders. I grinned like an idiot who didn't know what was going on.

Claire accepted our thanks with a lazy smile. Her dress looked like it was made from a crazy quilt, in Christmas colors, of course. Her sister Melanie wore a severe black dress straining at the seams. She threw Claire a poisonous look and said, "*I* brought some brownies from Big Tex."

Dianne murmured that we'd heard such good things about Big Tex. The extended family moved on to pay tribute to Mrs. Ly. The Ly children, Mark Loc and Chana Xuan, and their spouses were established in gold chairs on either side of the matriarch, affirming the royal vibe.

I asked Johnny once why he didn't use his Vietnamese name, like the rest of his family. He said that one of his early teachers misread *John Ky Ly* as *Johnny Ly*, and he decided to keep it. He shrugged and smiled. "I thought having a nickname meant people liked you. I was very young."

Right behind the Brandons came another big crew, five girl-friends in their thirties and twice as many kids, out for the most exciting entertainment Beauchamp had to offer on a Saturday afternoon in December. We shook hands and said names that no one would remember through the laughter. Their eyes zoomed from one to the other of us, obviously trying to identify who was with whom. Always willing to help, I beamed as I put one arm around Dianne and the other over Johnny's shoulders. Clueless to the end, Johnny hugged me back, and Dianne kicked my ankle, fortunately a glancing blow. I don't know what the girlfriend guests made of us, but I'm always happy to give people a few minutes' speculative entertainment.

The last woman in the group, trailing behind her friends, wasn't speculating, and I didn't catch the name she muttered. The seven-year-old boy bopping other kids from behind had to be hers, not only because of the lank brown hair they shared, but because his cheeky glances meant he knew she wouldn't rein him in. I had confidence in our elves, though. Sure enough, Candy, the youngest Cortez sister who never got enough opportunities to boss people around, grabbed his shirt and pulled him to the treats right before he decapitated the orchid plant. I was sorry to see it spared.

Johnny weaved through them just in time to welcome a straw-haired man maybe ten years older than us. He introduced himself as Kevin Dixon, Justice of the Peace and manager of the Beauchamp

Sonic Drive-in. He carried several cling-wrapped trays, including another batch of Big Tex brownies.

"I thought people might like to try Sonic's new holiday desserts," he confided. "And of course, Big Tex brownies. Everybody loves those." He cast an admiring look at Dianne, like anybody would.

"Looks great," I agreed and whisked through introductions.

"Justice of the Peace?" asked Johnny, baffled.

"Elected last year." He puffed with pride. "I always wanted to be a lawyer, but never could afford the schooling, so JP is the next best thing, I figure. They trained us for two weeks so we can judge property cases. Where should I put the food?"

I waved down the gallery, and a couple of Cortez cousins swooped in to capture the goodies. Kevin's face brightened at all the beauty.

Sometimes I think about dating a Cortez sister or cousin, but I always sober up.

Mrs. Ly's voice carried during a brief lull. "Elisa, I was so sorry to hear about your husband." She was leaning forward to talk to Sad Lady, who drooped even more.

"We thought the party would be good for her, to help her get in the Christmas spirit," declared The Girlfriends' ringleader, her long red fingernails sparkling with glitter and jewels. She put an arm around the sagging shoulders. "We'll get you something to eat and drink, and you'll perk right up."

"You know I don't eat anything at parties," Elisa said, cross.

Johnny watched the group. "I wonder if that's because of allergies. Maybe I should show her what we have."

"The elves will do that," consoled Dianne, putting her arm though his.

"That's Elisa Herald," whispered Kevin as he hauled out his phone and swiped. "Her husband died recently. It was terrible, my first death as Justice of the Peace. The police said I didn't have to come, that they'd tell me all about it, but that's not really doing the job, is it?"

Johnny looked bewildered. "What is the job exactly?"

"In rural counties, JPs pronounce people dead and decide if more investigation is needed," I said. "In urban areas, there's forensic staff for that."

"But Beauchamp is only twenty-two miles from Austin," exclaimed Johnny. "Don't the cities help the rural areas?"

"Sure." Glum, Kevin handed me his phone. "But you have to stand in line behind all Travis County deaths and all the other rural counties who've submitted their cases. Somebody has to decide on the spot."

When Dianne turned her head away, avoiding the corpse, I passed the phone over her to Johnny after scarcely a glance. It wasn't as bad as I feared, just somebody who looked asleep face up on the ground, although heads are usually rounder.

Johnny took the phone and stared. "He worked on the house! I liked him. It was important to him to create a safe, comfortable home. He was looking forward to meeting us. He was going to come by last Monday to meet Dianne."

"Contractors always say that, Johnny. About the good job," I explained, glancing around to see if Matt heard.

"Of course, but I watched him work too. He asked me about details, and came up with creative ways to do things, not just the fastest or cheapest. He always took safety precautions. Once he asked me to hold the ladder and spot him when his crew was at lunch." Johnny peered closer at the phone. "He was on the site alone, climbing in the frame by himself? It looks like a new subdivision."

"That's what everyone said," said Kevin. "But even careful people get careless at quitting time. He fell backwards from the roof and hit his head on a rock when he landed. A shame, but accidents happen."

"Do they?" asked Johnny as he handed back the phone. "Would you like an assistant? Someone to examine the dead bodies for you?"

Kevin sighed. "I would, and the budget allows for an assistant, but who would do that? The weddings and small claims court are the fun parts. Wait, you're volunteering? Really?"

Johnny nodded.

"You're a vet," I said, not liking this at all. Looking at dead bodies couldn't be good for anyone's mental health.

"Dead is dead across the species," said Johnny, with no expression. With only a sliver of pain in his voice, he added, "I got through forensics and pathology in zoo vet school. I would be happy to serve the community in this way." As Kevin moved on after thankfully accepting the offer, Johnny whispered, "JD, how does a restaurant manager become justice of the peace?"

"You heard him. You get elected. Then you get to run small claims court, perform weddings, and declare people dead. No worries. Like he said, they get two weeks of training."

While Johnny tried to make sense of Texas politics—hopeless— Matt Davies jumped in behind The Girlfriends. After a quick hug for his partner's wife Elisa the Sad Lady, he again demanded his check from Mrs. Ly.

We all raised our voices to greet the next people, but we could still hear him whining like a TV commentator. He'd done all he could; it was unreasonable to expect more; he'd take a cut in pay if he could just get his check and go. Mrs. Ly raised an eyebrow and agreed to fifteen percent less. Matt suggested three percent.

"Excuse me," murmured Dianne as she shook someone's hand and stepped back. "This is my jam."

In full elder-respect mode, she offered to calculate a fair number that took into account the delay in finishing and the cost of hiring someone else to finish the work, with the assistance of her *Tío* Pedro, who owned a construction company and was standing right over there. I wished I could pay more attention, but more people poured through the door. At last glance, Mrs. Ly was smiling, Matt wasn't, and Dianne, gaze modestly lowered, held the arm of a big, burly guy whose Latino genes and career in the sun had toasted him even darker than Matt. As he and Mrs. Ly discussed the punch list, it seemed likely that he would finish the work, at a special price, since it was for his *querida sobrina*.

"Dianne is wonderful," whispered Johnny in awe as she returned to us with a one-second flickering smile of triumph, leaving *Tío* Pedro in possession of the field. He marched Matt away like a drill sergeant, which he had been, Dianne told me later.

I scarcely had time to agree before the next arrival banged the front door open wide. We stepped back in lockstep as she stormed through, boots clattering.

SISTERS

"*T*hank you for coming, Sophie Thi," said Johnny. "I am sorry you missed the tour, but of course family can explore the house as they like."

"You think I want to see how you ruined the house?" she snapped.

She looked like an enraged Johnny, if such a thing were possible.

"Sister?" murmured Dianne.

I popped a nod in agreement.

"Thank you for bringing brownies," Johnny said, gesturing to her almost upside-down cling-wrapped tray. "Everyone thinks Big Tex's bakery is the best."

What everybody thinks is that the bakery inside the biggest grocery store within twenty miles is their only chance to purchase pastries other than the prepackaged bricks from C-stores along the highway. I drove all over Austin to buy the specialty treats.

She stomped away with a snarl. "I'll put the blasted brownies on the table."

"Your generosity overwhelms us, Sophie Thi," said Mrs. Ly in her best platoon-commanding voice.

The young woman drew her head down like a turtle, shoulders hunched, and trudged to a stop in front of her family.

"I wish they wouldn't do that," Johnny whispered, barely moving his lips.

Through her wide smile towards visitors traversing the front yard, Dianne whispered, "What?"

"Clearly my parents or grandmother, probably all, told her she had to show up today to support me." Johnny looked after his sister with a bleak expression. "It wasn't easy to have a weird brother. She begged to go to a private high school to get away from teachers and kids who knew me. Then when she wanted to go to an elite college, her college fund was mostly spent. Things went down below sea level from there, even after she went to Princeton on scholarship and loans."

I watched Mrs. Ly dress her granddaughter down, echoed by her father, both softly enough to look like a pantomime. As Sophie Thi slumped and scowled even more, I felt a reverse sympathy. I didn't go to my father's back-east alma mater; I wanted to be nearby because of Mother's cancer. I attended the University of Texas, no slacker school, on scholarship and loans because my father was too outraged to contribute.

I turned back to the door to prepare for the next group we had to welcome. Dianne wore her Brave Girl smile. Johnny looked ready for capital punishment, but he burst into smiles and dropped to his knees when a first grade–sized girl with fluffy black hair held up a tabby kitten. Johnny stroked its head with one finger. He always found cats easier than humans.

"What a pretty kitten you have," he said, the cat being the first guest he was truly happy to see.

"He's not ours. We can't keep him," snapped the father, another Nordic type fried in the Texas sun.

The mother, a larger version of her daughter, made a helpless gesture. "We found him by our house. I told her you might help the kitty."

"Of course I will," said Johnny, holding his hands out as the girl poured the kitten into them. "And you can come see him whenever you like."

The girl clapped her hands and jumped. "Mommy! Daddy! Did you hear?"

Face lightening in relief, the mother shoved a shrink-wrapped package at us. "And we brought some brownies from Big Tex."

Dianne thanked the giver with her trademark smile. She muttered to me as she held up the tray to signal an elf, "That's one cat."

"He might have brothers and sisters, or even a mommy. Can you show me where you found him?" Johnny looked up at the parents for permission.

"I can," piped the girl, waving her arm. "Right by our house, on the other side of the park."

"They've been crying for days," grouched the father.

"Only one night. You weren't home during the day when they were screaming," said the mother as they headed for the food, pausing only to glare at The Girlfriends as they passed each other.

Another entry for the feud category. As Johnny and his new friend set out for the park, two blocks across the street from Gregg House, I whispered to Dianne as we both eyed the brief conflict. "That's six cats. Or ten."

"*Madre de Dios*," she murmured or prayed.

As the trickle of guests turned into a tsunami, Dianne and I split the welcoming duties to avoid a bottleneck like rush hour on Austin's Colorado River Bridge. Guests fell into three categories: friends of Mrs. Ly, people who went to school with Johnny's father and aunt, and the rest of the population of Beauchamp and three surrounding towns. Previously the Beauchamp school system nurse, Mrs. Ly used her open house as her personal war on poverty. She targeted suffering families with substantial help, presented by a Vietnamese Santa who delighted in all festivals, anybody's festival, and everyone else could count on generous gift cards supporting local businesses (like Big Tex).

You could further divide our guests by relationships. Gawkers who'd never seen Gregg House before, who didn't know anyone, wandered around, staring. Others were thrilled to see their neighbors and possible friends amid flailing arms and air kisses. Feuds revealed themselves by scowls, abrupt turns, loud subject changes, and people bouncing away from others like matching-pole magnets.

In a half-hour that felt like half a year, Johnny returned, his arms full of kittens, his human companion skippety-hopping beside him.

She blasted down the hall, shouting, "Mommy, Daddy, we found three more! And I'm going to come over every day and take care of them!"

Dianne clasped her hands together in tender glee. "Look! A little white one with blue eyes! I'm going to name her Nevada."

That means "snowy," not a desolate desert state with the best marketing plan in the history of the universe.

Imagine twenty or so people saying something similar, depending on whether their taste ran to gingers, tabbies, tabbies with white socks, or, like Dianne, white cats, as Johnny plowed his way to his clinic door, halfway down the hall by the Christmas tree.

"Help me get them settled in their new home," he said to his small assistant as he held open the clinic door. Six more children barreled through, including Mariposa, camera clicking away at the kittens. It would have been seven kids, but Elisa Herald roused herself enough to grab her son's shoulder as she scowled.

Dianne and I kept on acting glad to meet people and accepting more delicacies. Everyone commented on the striking black orchids as they rifled through the cards and coupons. I stepped away while Dianne accepted the praise and explained that the black orchid had mystical meanings in Asia. Keeping a poker face took all my attention. When Johnny eventually returned, we deserted him to take the food back to the tables. We needed a break.

We collided with the elves, also armed with plates and saying, "Not *there!*" Dianne glanced back at Johnny. I took her plates and told her to go, and the elves left my sister Cherry to face off with me.

"What are you doing, feeding the whole town?" She scowled as she took over my offerings to distribute with hers.

One clattered, being real glass instead of plastic. I choked. That was Miss Leigh's plate, full of illegal goodies. I snatched the plate back as an eager young hand reached for one of the pretties. The small imp threatened a tantrum, and I pushed peppermint-covered brownies in its direction, though I doubted anything softer than an air raid siren would be heard.

I was wrong. The doorbell rang, and I instinctively moved in that direction.

Dianne swept the door open to reveal a policeman, complete with mirror shades (because this is Texas in winter). He was brown as Dianne and almost as tall, but born without smile muscles. The silver husky beside him grinned, blue eyes and flopping ears adding a maniacal touch.

"May I come in with my dog?" asked the officer in a way that didn't feel like a request.

Dianne's bright lipstick gleamed as she welcomed them both. "Of course! Working dogs are always welcome. I'm Dianne Cortez, and you are—" She leaned in to read his badge. "Officer Alejandro Quintanilla-Villenueva."

"Most people call me Officer Al. This is Cupcake. She's not so much working as training," explained the officer, proving he could smile, probably at Dianne's effortless pronunciation.

I jumped when I realized what I was holding. I power-marched into the kitchen.

Chantal was huddled by the pantry, giving herself an insulin shot. As she put away her equipment, she scolded, "I told Cherry to put those out."

"We can't." I glanced over my shoulder and saw Dianne step back to admit Officer Al and Cupcake. "Our neighbor brought them for Johnny."

"So? Johnny's never minded sharing."

"They're medicinal, and a drug dog just arrived," I hissed.

"For Johnny, Mr. Totally Straight and Narrowest of the Narrow?"

"Yes. Let me by." I grabbed a plastic bag from the pantry. I folded up the empty box sitting on the counter and shoved it and the whole plate in. Meanwhile, the policeman paid court to Johnny's grandmother.

"That's a huge dog!" Chantal exclaimed as she peered into the hall. "Where do we put this stuff?"

"Freezer? Behind the meat?"

"Will that work?" Chantal rummaged through the freezer, already full of bags of bacon, chicken *tinga*, ground beef, and other meats to spice up Johnny's vegetarian meals. He does most of the cooking because he likes it, and he tolerates what the rest of us do to it.

"Who knows?" I shoved the bag to the very back of the top freezer shelf.

"Not me."

The deed done, Chantal and I scrubbed our hands under a cascade of hot water and suds. While trying to remember if the police could arrest the whole party on drug charges for one box of edibles, I took exactly one step into the gallery to meet doom when doom met me from another direction. My father tapped my sleeve.

"JD, have you met Harold Bucholz, mayor of Beauchamp?"

Like a trained seal, I stuck my hand out to the youngish man—somewhere between my father's age and mine—who wore a dark suit with picks of subtle lavender, emphasized by his lavender tie. I was ready to lie and say "Of course," but he interrupted with a bark of laughter.

"I came through the back door, so I skipped the receiving line. Mrs. Ly's my old friend and partner in community service. We're sorry she's leaving, but your father gives you quite a reference, as you might expect."

A beat late, I laughed at the joke. I wouldn't expect that at all.

"What brings you to Beauchamp?" he asked.

Recognizing my elevator speech cue, I replied, "I've always wanted to bring the law out of the boardroom and beyond the courtroom into people's everyday lives, into current events as they unfold. What kinds of issues does Beauchamp grapple with?

The mayor nodded, pleased. "I think all Texas towns face immigration issues these days."

"That's a particular passion of mine," I enthused. "I've grown up with family stories of how my ancestors came over with nothing but memories from the Old Country, lots of old countries, and worked their way up. My great-grandfather was first-generation Irish-American and the first Thompson to go to college. He put himself through school picking cotton."

Mayor Bucholz did the usual double-take of people when they discover that white people also picked cotton, even if they had more of a choice about it.

"That first James Thompson became not only a civil rights attorney but a judge. Because my ancestors were shown mercy and opportunities, I want to help others in the same way."

I'd lost my audience. The horror on both their faces told me that we viewed immigrant problems differently. On our first tour around the town, Johnny pointed out Beauchamp's second largest house, the mayor's house, a modern brick ranch structure half the size of Gregg House, and now I wanted to ask who built it, whether every worker was a citizen or legal resident. But I knew it wasn't the moment for activism. I also knew not to mention my other legal passions, those being defense (public or otherwise) and unions. Maybe I should talk about Multi-ABBA. I settled for, "What kind of industries are attracted to Beauchamp?" But since the answer was basically none— Elrod up the road towards Austin got all the new businesses—conversation withered. I blithered my thanks and directed him to his good friend Mrs. Ly.

I answered my father's seething glare by grabbing a dessert plate and saying, "Have a brownie. Oops, there's Dianne waving at me."

She was indeed, reminding me why I love her. I scooted out of the cast iron frying pan and into the firenado to meet her and the policeman by the bathroom door.

FATHERS AND MOTHERS

*D*ianne broke off the Spanish-fest to say, "JD, this is Officer Al and Cupcake."

"Very glad to meet both of you." I shook his hand and eyed Cupcake. I didn't trust her not take my arm off, despite the friendly invitation in her eyes. "Did someone call you? I hope we weren't too loud." The Gregg House land took up its own block, and the mansion was far enough from all other houses that we could hold a rave without bothering the neighbors, but I was trying for innocence, pretending he brought his pet instead of a drug dog.

Officer Al, young and sincere, assured me, "Oh, no. Even if you were, all your neighbors are here anyway. My *tía* lives in Beauchamp, and she's brought me to Mrs. Ly's Christmas party since I was—well, I don't remember ever not coming here. I thought it would be a good chance for Cupcake to get used to a crowd."

"Ah," I said, trying not to make that word a sigh of relief.

Just then a man exited the bathroom, and we all stepped back, except Cupcake, who sat at attention in the doorway. The man edged backwards, looking worried.

Officer Al's terra cotta cheeks turned brighter. "Come on, Cupcake. Don't block the path."

"Let me show you the food," said Dianne. "I'm sure our partner Dr. Ly has something for Cupcake too."

They proceeded down the hall to a chorus of children exclaiming, "Doggy!" with an official explanation that the doggy was working. Not buying that, the doggy happily nuzzled any nearby hand. I stuck my head in the bathroom and sniffed, I hoped discreetly. Cupcake's nose is better than mine, but I didn't smell any drugs. At least the bleach odor was faint now.

I ambled back to the front door in search of Johnny. I hoped he'd bribe the officer of the law—the dog, that is, with enough treats to keep her from doing her job.

I didn't find him, and I welcomed and directed another half-dozen people before I heard my father's brisk, staccato steps.

"JD, I have to leave." My father had that sharp-eyed look that meant a slice-and-dicing for somebody. I wasn't being paranoid to think it was me. "We haven't had a chance to talk."

That's the way I like it. Imitating every elder statesman I'd ever seen, some of them up close and personal, I gave a slow, gracious nod. "Thank you for coming. Perhaps you'd like to see my office?" I stepped towards into my office and jiggled the latch under the door gate. As the office gate opened, I spread a hand in welcome as I stepped inside. I wanted him to see me in a real lawyer's office, not the cubes and open offices of Corporations R Our Meal Ticket, LLC. "Are the grandparents going back with you?"

"They have their own car. Besides, they're going back to Waco." His gaze strafed the room.

I was proud of its old-school look, furniture even older than the 1940s antiques in the rest of the house, but still in the dark red mahogany theme. Barrister's bookcases with their heavy leaded glass fronts covered every bare wall. The heavy glass obscured my law books and literature class texts. The wingback client chairs were from the forties, but their Danish design with crushed red velvet channels fit with the older furniture. I had them shoved close together to make space for a massive globe, its countries and oceans faded to shades of brown. Useless as a reference after the political landscape scrambled itself post–World War II, it normally sits in the gallery, but it's also a drinks cabinet, if you lift the top of the globe. So it had to go behind a gate.

My office now reminded me of my great-grandfather's. I have only hazy memories of it before he retired and the family helped him close shop. Someone gave me his prism-shaped name plate to play with and plunked me in the window seat overlooking the Houston skyline. I turned the plate over and over, marveling at the dull, smooth wood on two sides that contrasted with the other side of gleaming gold, or goldish. I traced the engraved letters. It was my name too: James Thompson. I was too young to read the words after that.

My father, visibly unimpressed with my re-creation of our ancestor's office, stared out one of the windows that ringed the circular room. I doubted he was admiring the crepe myrtles, their branches reaching for the sky in desperate supplication. Beyond the bare trees, Matt the contractor and Dianne's uncle argued, but that wasn't relevant to my interests.

I waited, marveling at how childhood dread can leap up into a full-grown frame, remembering other days when my father stood with his back to me, forcing me to imagine the emotions I couldn't see on his face. I was staring down the maw of thirty years, now taller than he, but I felt like I was eight.

He whirled around. "I can't believe what you said to the mayor. You ruined your chances there, and I haven't seen one other potential client in this whole motley crew. Immigration! How do you intend to make a living? This is as bad as when you wanted to be a union attorney."

My ears still burned from the laughter when I announced that desire at the Thanksgiving table. "In Texas, boy?" said every last one of the Thompson attorneys.

Now I wished I could squirt the fire extinguisher on the metaphorical flames blasting from my father's mouth. I leaned against a windowsill opposite him, the massive desk between us. "I can forward you my business plan, if you're interested in investing."

My father snort-growled his opinion of my worth as an investment. "Who owns this furniture? This house? Not you."

I replied, matching his fire with ice. "I am renting from Mrs. Ly, like you rent your office in Houston."

"Not the same at all. Your grandfather got you an internship and then a clerkship with Judge Pereira. You didn't want that, so I got you the job you just quit."

"Thank you," I said, dropping the temperature lower. "And here I thought it might have been due to my class standing and position on the Law Review."

"You quit both those positions to be a small-town ambulance chaser. You've thrown away everything, including the Jaguar."

My back stiffened like the rebar Matt and Dianne's uncle were fighting about. "Excuse me. You made a down payment—a generous one, I admit—but between its payments and my student loans, I could have bought a house. So now I'm renting a house and office and driving a car that's paid for. I assumed the Jag was mine to do with as I wished, even wrap it around a tree like my cousin did with his graduation present."

Some might have called the noise he made a laugh. "That's a low bar to get over."

"More like a trench," I acknowledged.

"And now you're back to living with your idiot roommates from college." He fumed, beyond words for a sadly short time. Then he reloaded. "Why don't you decide which one you want and get married?"

I don't know if my face turned white or red, though I could have checked in the oval antique mirror on the back of the door. I took the deep breaths that meditation teachers recommend. Those breaths shouldn't sound like a bull panting. I reminded myself that I could be the better person. What a stupid idea.

"What if it's both?" I drawled.

That sent him charging right out the front door.

I carefully shut the office door and leaned against it to consider my next move. The globe with its now fictional map called to me from deep inside, where the bourbon lived. My friends had already loaded the cabinet with their favorite beverages and, touchingly, mine. With a silent toast to them, I poured myself a drink.

Slamming the door open, Dianne rushed in and grabbed my drink. She gulped it down and sagged against my desk. "I so needed that," she murmured, her usual alto even throatier.

I waited for an explanation with a sympathetic look.

She lifted one hand to her forehead—a nice *pietá* pose, that mother-of-dead-Jesus-look. "My mother has made friends with and pressed her card on—to be fair, mine too—even the faintest Latinx-looking person here."

"Of course she did," I soothed as I poured another drink for myself. "She's a successful businesswoman, like you."

"You'll think that when she's here putting on a *quinceañera* every other weekend? But that's not the worst. She bagged the priest."

She reached for my new drink, but I took a large swallow before she could get her hands on it. "Let me make something you like." In a tumbler, I mixed rum and Pepsi Whatever-Their-Low-Cal-Drink-Is-Called-This-Week. The drinks globe holds multitudes. Who cares what its map says?

She took several swigs before continuing. "She asked him to bless the house—an event she would be glad to arrange, of course—and I said Mrs. Ly's Jewish and it wouldn't be appropriate. My mother pulled Johnny over to ask him, and Father Emilio said he knew a rabbi from some Austin interfaith group and they could do a joint cere-mony. Johnny said that would be great, they could install a *mezuzah*, whatever that is."

"You remember. That little tube that he put on his door at Casa Cortez. I think it has scriptures in it."

"Yes! I was afraid we wouldn't get our security deposit back because of it. And then Johnny asked if the interfaith group could also send a Buddhist to honor his grandfather. JD, now the priest and the whole town will be telling Mother whether I'm attending Mass, and if I wanted that, I'd set up shop back in Garland, Texas." She tossed back the rest of her drink while I tried to untangle that sentence. "JD, do you mind if I tell my mother you're gay? Because she's back to looking at me with those tragic if-only eyes, with the tiniest sob in her voice every time she speaks to me."

"Close to what my father just called me. Said I should decide if I wanted to marry you or Johnny."

Dianne looked shocked. "That's unbrilliant. I guess you could be bisexual, though I've never noticed. Do you want me to talk to him?"

"He's gone. Besides, I told him both."

She clapped her hands in delight. "That's it! I'll tell her I can't decide!"

"Don't blame me when you end up married to Johnny." Because she and I really have settled the question of our marriage, as in never.

She made that little sound like she's choking back laughter, perfected in years of Catholic school. "I guess it wouldn't work. You'll send out invitations to your and Carolyn's wedding—"

I deepened my voice to its most mature and said, "Carolyn and I decided we weren't up for a long-distance relationship."

Dianne's eyebrows rose to form delicate arches. "She lives twenty-five miles away."

"Thirty since she moved to Cedar Park. Or is it Leander? Maybe Volente? Somewhere northwest of Austin. Anyway, we got to the point where across the street was too far." To swerve off the topic, I asked, "What about Whatsis Name? Can't remember—"

"It's irrelevant." She tilted her chin and glared at me. "We disagreed about the best time to bring your girlfriend home to meet your family, me thinking four or five months at the outside, him thinking the twelfth. As in 'of never.' I mean, you and I dated less than six weeks when you brought me to your home."

"Special circs," I protested. "Believe me, now I take it 'Andante,

Andante.' But it was fall break, my mother had cancer, and I knew that meeting my girlfriend would make her happy. What kept her going as long as she did was clawing her way to the next big occasion. Remember those bridal magazines we found in her room after she died? They weren't for the twins, unless she was looking at flower girl outfits. Made my blood run cold—I mean, we weren't even twenty. But she always looked ahead."

Dianne made some kind of sound deep in her throat. It's amazing how many sounds Catholic school graduates make without opening their mouths. Someone should document the language. "You wanted your mother to meet me as soon as possible because it would make her happy. In the same situation, Cole would figure he'd never have to bring his Latina girlfriend home."

"Idiot. Him." I couldn't think of what else to say, so, after my usual second's delay while I considered whether I'd do the same for Chantal, I held out my arms for Dianne to fall into. After her usual second's delay while she decided whether she'd do so for Johnny, she stumbled forward. She held on to my waist and hummed the song I named. I joined in with my part. Someone humming against your chest is a good feeling. Her sequined poinsettia fascinator was sticking me right under the eye, but I hoped my humming into her hair felt as good to her.

"What's wrong with this picture?" she muttered into my shirt after two choruses.

"You mean how we're hiding and drinking and Johnny's out there being a host?"

She pushed herself upright. "Yeah, that."

She checked her hair and makeup in the door mirror. As she smoothed down her dress, I felt a nostalgic pang for all the times we sneaked away and had to rearrange ourselves before rejoining the occasion. I checked my shirt for lipstick.

She left the room with a delicate wobble, even in ballerina flats. Dianne does not believe in uncomfortable shoes. I admired the view and sighed for what might have been and what used to be before I followed.

As I stepped out of my office, the visiting Casa Cortez contingent swarmed me. I noticed the townsfolk giving side eye to Jia and Shanice with their hands laced. I scooped up one in each arm to smack a kiss on each cheek. Rosemary came down the middle and threw her arms around my neck. All in all, it was more physical affection than I'd had in—none of your business.

Rosemary cooed her thanks for the hypoallergenic food I provided (even though Johnny issued the orders), and the others insisted we'd all get together soon.

Then a squeaky voice piped from below, "Smile!" Little Mariposa snapped a photo and ran off.

"That looks like Dianne's old camera," said Jia. "Remember how she'd drag us to some Austin tourist attraction so she could take photos to send to her great-grandmother? Even then everybody had phone cameras."

"That's Dianne," I agreed, having figured as "*mi novio*" in some of those photos. "And that is her camera, also her cousin."

"She said you'll do this open house every year, and I said we should also have the Casa Cortez winter reunion then. She thought it was a great idea!"

"It is," I agreed. For years, Dianne's sent out invitations to dinner every quarter (automatically through her mail program), with attendance ranging from her and me to nearly twenty.

Rosemary, Jia, and Shanice laughed as they left, calling good wishes all the way to their car.

I sighed. Imitating my father, I surveyed the hall for potential clients. Maybe some of these happy families would be divorcing soon, and I could guide them to a mediated divorce rather than a full-scale war. Shoving that happy holiday thought aside, I reminded myself that I was single and should be looking for potential partners, even temporary ones, but that was a lost cause.

Besides, I could hardly look for new partners when I needed to keep an eye on my sisters. Old habits die hard. I could hear Cherry's actor's voice projecting from near the piano as she encouraged Grandmother to have a peppermint chocolate cookie and take a break from performing. Merry was closer, near the Christmas tree, but I couldn't hear her because she's not an actor. She wore a pleasant smile as she pressed a gift envelope into Sad Lady Elisa Herald's slack hands. Merry's smile hardened as the son grabbed at the candy canes in her elf apron pocket. Mind you, she was trying to hand him one, but some people think assault is more fun than a gift.

The twins didn't seem to be in danger, and they seemed cheerful, but girls have to sparkle more, it seems. My Christmas spirit died with my mother in the fall of my college sophomore year. Cancer or no cancer, she always threw a Christmas-palooza, and the first year without her was a bleak contrast.

Everyone at Casa Cortez invited me to their family celebrations that year, but I went home—later than I could have, earlier than I wanted to—for my ten-year-old sisters' sake. I arrived home to glum faces and mournful silence. Thinking about a Christmas light tour, like we used to do with Mother, I asked where they'd like to go, but Cherry said, "Anywhere it's not Christmas."

So we went to Alfred's Kosher Deli and munched pastrami sandwiches amid blue foil stars and dreidels while I strained for conversation that could continue beyond one volley. ("How's school?" "Scouts?" "Piano?" "Fine," one twin would say while the other sighed.) Eventually I came up with, "Is there anything you really want for Christmas?" They looked at each other, their sandwiches, and crosseyed down their drink straws before raising their eyes to meet mine and blurting, "We want bras." Things got worse from there.

They've grown beyond needing a brother for anything but moving their belongings, but I still watch out for them (and we go back to Alfred's every year for a non-Christmas meal). Now I thought about helping Merry with her pest, but, still smiling, she got him in a headlock while Elisa, hand over her heart, gasped at her gift. Mrs. Ly had no doubt justified her reputation yet again. Elisa suddenly became aware of her son's behavior, probably because of the screeching, and she made a limp effort to calm him down. Merry shoved most of her candy canes into his hands and swished away to bestow largesse on another family, leaving Elisa looking broken and the son shoving candy canes into his mouth.

Merry's next family was the kitten rescuers, and the little girl jumped with glee over her candy cane and gift card. Her parents gave it a cursory glance before glaring at Elisa Herald and son. I wondered what was going on there.

I gave up trying take my father's advice. I can't look at people as stepping stones to my goals. I returned to my usual method of fascination with the variety of people on the planet and their myriad ways of coping. Grandmother's music twinkled back to me, and I remembered her rewrite of Billy Joel's "Piano Man" as "Piano Girl" for her various gigs with similar commentary, though mostly I was too young to understand.

"Now Tom by the bar is no friend of mine; he brought me two drinks or three," she crooned.

And now I do the same, taking the song back to "Piano Man," as I observe those around me, the guy pursuing the woman who keeps moving away, every exclamation over the incredible black orchid plant, Dianne's younger brother Zap as chief tour guide, and all the doe-eyed women who'd been on his tour five times, he being the male version of Dianne. I wondered how many times he'd tried to answer the question, "Why Black Orchid Enterprises?"

Zap deepened his voice and emphasized each word, trying to sound like he knew what he was talking about. "Black orchids are an Asian symbol for very deep symbolism, very magical, you know."

I could hear his effort to avoid saying that the Black Orchid was his sister's favorite superhero, there not being many choices in her younger years. And me? After Johnny and Dianne agreed on something, even for wildly different reasons, I went along rather than prolong the discussion *cum* argument. I stepped further away from Zap in hopes he wouldn't ask me to explain further.

I joined Johnny, looking fascinated, in a conversation with a group of gardeners recruiting others to raise vegetables for the Beauchamp All-Vegetable Orchestra. Johnny promised to grow and contribute. After I admitted to playing trombone in high school (because all the cute girls were in band and it's hard to meet anyone when you play the piano), they debated the most trombone-like vegetable.

They had the choice narrowed to a trombetta squash or long bottle gourd when a choking sound by the special diets table made us all look that way.

WONDER DOG

*E*lisa Herald gagged as she turned bright red. She fumbled with her shoulder bag, but couldn't get it open. "Epi," she choked.

In an instant, Johnny and I were at her side. I tossed her purse to Dianne and helped Johnny ease Elisa to the floor.

"I'm not finding an Epipen," said Dianne. "But her car insurance is here. 2010 Camry, JBR3495."

"On it," said Chantal, heading for the back door.

Dianne tossed the keys to Chantal and kept digging.

"I've got one in the clinic," said Johnny, leaving me with the choking patient.

I grabbed Elisa's hand and told her everything was okay. That was inane, but either everything would be okay, or it wouldn't matter.

Dianne reached for her own phone and tapped three numbers. "Ambulance," she said. "Food allergy, anaphylactic shock. 709 Louisiana Street. Beauchamp." She studied the plate in her hand and frowned. "I would have said 'peanuts,' but the food she was eating is labeled 'No Nuts.'" She picked at the tape that fastened the card. The ends of the tape were crumpled and curled.

The other guests froze into zombie-like expressions. Maybe they never had medically challenged roommates.

Johnny and Chantal returned at the same time.

"No pen," she said.

Johnny held up a box. As he readied the pen, he commanded, "JD, stabilize her."

As the tallest and heaviest, that had to be my job. It's good to be useful. I straddled her thighs, and Johnny jabbed the pen into the one nearest him. She jerked so hard that I had to grab the table to keep my balance.

Heavy steps, one foot dragging, announced Nurse Ly. She barely apologized as she pushed through the gawkers. "Wash her mouth out, John Ky. She could still have some of the allergen there."

Most people backed away, but one of my sisters pushed through. That alone told me it was Merry. She was majoring in bio-eco something and didn't mind organics as much as other people.

"Can I help?" she asked.

"Bag up what she was eating," Johnny instructed. "Bring some water, paper towels, and gallon-size plastic bags."

Merry flew into the kitchen.

Dianne's event-planning mother barreled through the crowd. She embraced her eldest child as Dianne bent down to put her head on her mother's shoulder.

"Can I do something, Lupita?" her mother asked in feather-soft tones.

Chantal stepped in. "Get everybody on the other side of the house so the doctor can work. JD, play us some carols."

I glanced at the patient one more time. Her mouth was swelling like a double lip injection.

Mrs. Ly said, "It can take the ambulance fifteen minutes to get this far out. Do you have tubing you could use to keep her airway open?"

Johnny said, "Yes. Merry, it's in—"

His sister Sophie Thi wandered into view and shrieked, "Oh my God! What's he doing?" She crumpled to the floor.

I crashed down on the piano keys, the way no one ever allowed me to, and hollered with Chantal, "Dashing through the snow!" while Johnny's father and uncle brought in an Asian screen from one of the downstairs bedrooms to set around the medical scene. Mrs. Cortez assembled a wall of sisters and cousins to contain our guests with a zone defense. Mariposa darted around the room, butterflies bouncing and camera clicking.

I thumped and shout-sang for a year, or maybe fifteen minutes. Dianne joined us, taking over some of the melodies to let Chantal's silvery voice dart into high descants. I heard a thread or two of grudging audience participation, less than for the usual sing-along request, but after all, someone might be dying on the other side of the screen. Elisa's friend, the one who insisted she come today, had an arm around Elisa's son and stood as close as the elves would let her, simultaneously trying to see what was going on but keeping the boy from disturbing sights. They didn't join the singing.

Johnny's father and uncle trudged back through at a "St. James Infirmary" speed, bearing the unconscious Sophie Thi on a folded screen. Great. Now we had two patients. Her grandmother walked beside her, one hand on her shoulder. Mrs. Ly shoved her walker ahead with her other hand. I charged into a martial "It Came Upon a Midnight Clear."

A firetruck full of paramedics and sirens put the final stake in our musical efforts. Chantal and I threw up our hands at the same time. The children ran to the windows to gawk, their parents right behind, pretending to corral their offspring. The Cortez-Thompson wall kept them on the piano side of the hall, leaving the paramedics a clear path through the door.

Half our crew surged forward to bribe the guests with food and drink; the other half, with fame and fortune as they snapped their phone cams "for our scrapbook and maybe publicity, so please hold up a sign with your name and contact info in case we have to contact you for permission," Cherry said. Other assistants handed out paper and markers for signs. Super. No chance I'd get out of doing social media for a lack of material.

I edged behind the line to Dianne, a grim goddess who didn't need a flaming sword. "Alive?" I whispered.

She jerked a nod. I let out a long breath. We dance-stepped in unison to let the gurney rattle through. I thrust aside the image of the paramedics as Day-Glo pallbearers.

Chantal grabbed us both. "Johnny's here now. Let's close with 'Happy New Year.'"

She tried to pull us back to the music area but collided with the kitten girl pulling her dad toward Elisa's friend and son. Dad was big enough not to argue with, so I stepped aside. Besides, I was curious, after the day's tension between the two families.

"I hope your mom's okay," said the girl to the boy. She looked up at her dad. "Let's go now."

I looked down at the slight sob from the person next to me, the girl's mother.

She pressed a napkin to her lips. "She wanted to do that. It was all her idea. He's picked on her ever since his father died, and I know we have to be understanding, but you can't have your kid bullied, you know? Not that the school helped."

I made a sound that she accepted as agreement but was really me choking on memories of the twins after Mother died, Cherry hog-wild and a menace, and no one seeing Merry's deep descent inside herself.

"And now she—kids are so much better than grownups, don't you think?" The mother blinked away tears.

"Can be," I agreed as Dianne and Chantal dragged me to the piano. I was still floating in long ago, on Cherry's 458th trip to the school counselor (this time for beating up older boys at recess), when she demanded, "Why doesn't anybody care about my sister?"

With Dianne pushing me down on the piano bench and Chantal shout-whispering in my ear, I had to return to the present so that we could go back to our oldest ABBA roots. We belted out that song about neighbors and friends and closing out the year, the one we've closed every December concert with. Our audience took the song as a cue to leave, thinning the ranks as we sang. They looked like deflated balloons ready to join the song's party detritus on the floor.

Officer Al returned from seeing the ambulance off, Cupcake bouncing at his heels.

Johnny cut his last note short to pursue the policeman. Cupcake helped by again sitting at attention in front of the half-open bathroom door. This time Officer Al eyed her with a doubtful expression.

"Officer, should I give the evidence to you?" asked Johnny.

"Evidence?" he asked, looking sadder the longer he studied his dog.

"I'm convinced the lady was poisoned."

He frowned. "What? She's allergic to peanuts. She accidentally ate something that had them."

"She ate something from the special diets table—things I curated and checked several times today—I guess not often enough—"

Officer Al broke in over Johnny's lament. "I need to step outside and play with Cupcake a minute. She thinks she's doing her job, and I have to reward her. That's her paycheck."

He pulled a stuffed snake toy from his belt and shook it front of Cupcake as he moved towards the back door. "Who's a good girl then? Who's Daddy's smart girl?"

When he and the smart girl made it through the back door, our remaining few guests parted like the Red Sea as the smart girl jumped and snapped at her dancing toy. I dashed into the bathroom and sniffed. Okay, my worst fear wasn't true, that some guest had puffed illegally. I checked all possible storage places, including the toilet tank, but didn't see anything obvious. I thought we could claim plausible deniability, even if Cupcake busted us. At least she wasn't pointing to the freezer.

I joined my friends at the back windows to watch Cupcake cash her check. She leaped high, snapping while Officer Al twirled the plush snake over his head. When that got old, he let it fly into the weeds. Cupcake bounced past it and grabbed something else, something like a rope. I caught my breath as Chantal screamed.

Not a rope.

A snake. A real danger noodle, a rattler, as near as I could make out with Cupcake whipping it up and down, pounding its head on the ground.

Officer Al looked bewildered, unsure how to intervene, or if he should.

People inside had no doubts. With everyone screaming "Snake!" half of them ran toward the front of the house; half ran toward the back. I don't remember giving my feet orders, but somehow I was at the front of the second group and shouting, "It's a rattler! Don't go near it."

Amid the screams, Johnny, all elbows, shoved through the crowd and past me as he shouted to Officer Al to call off Cupcake.

He tried, but Cupcake ignored him, never pausing in her snake-thrashing. Finally she danced back and slapped the snake on the flagstones. Officer Al jumped back when she laid it at his feet. It looked like a long, skinny bag of jelly. Proud and happy, Cupcake hopped around him and her trophy.

Johnny trotted down the back porch stairs and leaned over to examine Cupcake's prize. I called out a mantra from my Boy Scout days, "It's still got venom when it's dead. If it's dead. Either way, best not to touch it."

"I'm not going to," said the policeman, still backing off. "I'm calling Animal Control."

Johnny ignored us and tried to ignore Cupcake, still prancing with pride. He carried a gym bag, a white kitchen trash bag, and the Granny Grabber we joked about needing because our ceilings, closets, and cabinets now extended up to cloud level, beyond even my reach. He bowed his head like I'd seen him do for ten years, when he'd demand that someone turn the car around to check on a squashed animal beside the road. Either Scouting or vet school taught him about dead snakes, because he tenderly lifted the snake in the grabber tongs at arm's length and set it in the trash bag that he'd made into a careful open nest. Officer Al made it clear he was not going to help.

The policeman yelled into his phone loud enough for me to hear inside, over my swooning guests. "Look, you're Animal Control. I've got an animal that needs controlling. It's dead. No, that's not the same as armadillos on the highway. It's a danger to the public."

Still using the grabber, Johnny picked up the trash bag by its handles and deposited it in the gym bag. With the bag zipped and the snake contained, he held out his hand for the officer's phone. He spoke too softly for me to hear, especially with Dianne yelling as she lunged through the crowd, "Tell him he can't bring that snake in the house."

"Dianne says no snakes in the house," I called. "You'll have to give it the kiss of life outside."

Johnny, now squatted in front of Cupcake, waved a hand to indicate he'd heard. As near as I could tell, he was praising her for protecting her person, however sad he was at the outcome. He then stood in that boneless way he learned from two decades of martial arts training and took the gym bag to his grandfather's meditation room out back. Cupcake and Officer Al went the other direction, up the back porch stairs and into the house.

The few guests who remained pelted the policeman with questions: Was it a poisonous snake? Were the owners going to do something about this danger to the community? Accepting the angry glances that came my way, I went into full placation mode, saying that we'd try, though my plans involved signs that read "This property protected by attack snakes" to keep everyone away. The next question was, why wasn't it hibernating?

Johnny caught up with us at this point and explained in more detail than anyone wanted that snakes don't hibernate, though they slow down in winter. He pointed out that on an acre of undeveloped land, some nature was bound to creep in. Even more people headed out the front door.

His audience gone, Johnny returned to his previous topic with Officer Al. "I'd like to turn over evidence of Elisa Herald's poisoning.

She ate a Big Tex brownie with peanut butter smeared on the bottom. I could smell it, even though it was pressed in hard so you wouldn't get your hands gooey handling the brownie. It was made at a facility that handles nuts, but someone wasn't taking any chances. They rewrapped the brownies, taped one of the "Nut Free" tags on the plate, and set it on the special diets table. I saved all that. And our assistants took photos and recorded the contact information of everyone here for you to interview them. Someone must have seen something."

"I can't just open an investigation like that," he said, looking harassed. Cupcake pawed at his leg. He looked at her and sighed. "I have to take Cupcake outside again. I'll try the front yard this time."

"Why does your dog keep sitting in front of the bathroom?" Johnny asked. "This is the third time she's done it."

I closed the partially open door and said in a voice full of virtue, "I didn't find any evidence of drugs. Is she pulling your leg?"

The policeman shook his head. "She's not a drug dog. She's a cadaver dog, trained to find corpses."

EVIDENCE

I cranked my casual-interest voice to eleven. "She thinks there's a corpse in the bathroom? I mean, I just looked."

"The corpse doesn't have to be there," said Johnny. "Cadaver dogs are trained to smell the putrescence associated with human death. It's so pervasive that they assist archaeologists at ancient burial sites. I don't know what she could be detecting though. My grandparents lived here for almost fifty years, and my grandfather died in the hospital."

Officer Al unholstered his plush snake with a sigh. "I don't know. Her previous owner sold her to me for twenty dollars because Cupcake wouldn't work unless she felt like it, and the day she jumped in the lake with the water dogs was the last straw. She was supposed to be searching the forest. I really praise her when she works, in hopes she'll want to do it more. I know you're not supposed to change their training, but I'm trying her out on general police dog work. Maybe she'll like that better."

Someday I hope someone looks at me like Officer Al looked at Cupcake.

"Surely something's died here in that time," said Dianne, arms clutched tight around her middle. "Bugs, mice. And how could anyone smell anything besides the bleach?"

Johnny and Officer Al shook their heads in concert.

"The smell of human death is different from any other," said Johnny. "Very hard to eradicate, even though people can't smell it."

"Bleach," said the officer thoughtfully.

Dianne nodded and sniffed. "It was overpowering when we moved in. It's better, but still—"

"Bleach," said Johnny, deep in thought, his eyes gazing into some distant land. "Are you going to get a warrant to investigate?"

Officer Al's face flamed. "I—well—I can't. Nobody believes Cupcake. Even the judge has heard about her."

I nodded. "The dog who cried 'Corpse' once too often."

"Not exactly like that." He squirmed. "But every time she's had a chance to show them what she can do, she wouldn't. I need real evidence."

"But you can't search a residence without permission," I stated.

Johnny looked at the dog with affection. "She sounds like a cat. You can train cats to do amazing things. But usually they won't. I used to play fetch with my cat, but my sister always said I was lying. Sophie Thi had to believe after the surveillance camera showed Lotus fetching, but then she was mad because her cat Pho wouldn't do it. He would for me, but I never told her."

Officer Al's face was going to catch fire if it got any redder. "I know this is strange, but would you mind if I check? Cupcake seems awfully certain. If I don't find any confirmation, we can forget about it."

"It's my grandmother's house," said Johnny, folding his arms over his chest. "She might not appreciate that you'd investigate on Cupcake's say-so but not mine."

Johnny's grandmother, watching from her red throne a few feet away, wore a foreboding expression.

Officer Al swallowed. "Okay, I'll look at what you've got, but I can't promise anything else. Come with me to ask your grandmother's permission. She scares me."

Mrs. Ly eyed Cupcake. "So you brought this dog into my home to search for evidence of a crime?"

"No, ma'am. I take her everywhere I'm allowed to. She thinks there was a corpse in the bathroom, which sounds just as weird to me as it does to you, but I'd like to confirm it, if that's okay. Unofficially." He stopped for breath. "I'll accept whatever limits you want to place on me. If she's right, then I'll have to get official."

Mrs. Ly looked at me.

Another chance to show my legal skills! Maybe I wouldn't bomb this one. I pontificated, "As an attorney, I'd say that you don't have to let him do anything without a warrant. As your tenant who's going to be living in this town for a while, I'd suggest that unless you know of a good reason not to, you might consider allowing him to check out only the bathroom, since that's the area of interest."

"You can do that?" asked Chantal, astonished. "Say he can't look at anything but the bathroom? I thought once they were inside, they could do anything."

"That's vampires," I whispered.

"I'll accept the bathroom," said Officer Al. "That's where she keeps pointing."

"You want to help the dog, don't you, Grandmother?" asked Johnny. "Don't try to pet her. She's working."

Mrs. Ly pulled her hand back. "I've seen you walking down the street with your dog, young man. Are you from this town?"

"I have to walk her a lot. She has so much energy. I can count on her eating another pillow for every hour I work over my regular shift."

"Stop getting pillows?" suggested Dianne.

"Then she starts on the bed and the couch. I hope I can get a new mattress with my tax refund. But no, ma'am, I'm from Elrod."

At mention of the neighboring town that somehow got all the advantages that poor cousin Beauchamp didn't, Mrs. Ly looked as disapproving as she would if Cupcake dumped a load on the red carpet (not that she would, being a Very Good Dog).

"But my *tía*—my cousin, really, Renata Flores, but she's the same age as my mother—has lived here most of her life."

"Renata! I shall certainly ask her about you. I've worked with Renata on many community projects." After aiming a menacing eye at him, Mrs. Ly's face relaxed into a smile. "I'll follow my lawyer's suggestions and allow you to investigate the bathroom."

Great. Now I was on the list of people to blame. But she said "my lawyer." Figure of speech?

Officer Al, followed by his faithful companion, went to his car and brought back a small black bag, maybe his emergency crime kit.

"How are you going to test Cupcake's hypothesis?" asked Johnny, hard on the policeman's heels as he entered the bathroom.

I followed too, as Mrs. Ly's legal representative, though I wasn't sure I'd get a billable hour out of it. Okay, I wanted to see too, and Johnny and I could keep him from going elsewhere in the house.

"Shut the door," said Officer Al as he closed the window and its blinds.

I winched my eyes shut when he flipped on his flashlight, actually a blacklight. I felt like there should be music playing, but dancing with two other guys in a bathroom never figured in my dreams.

"Ah," said Johnny. "I thought you'd do a chemical test."

"We will, but this is a quick check for body fluids." Al's voice sounded distracted.

I frowned. "This being a bathroom, body fluids are guaranteed."

"Blood's different. It's dark, not neon."

And so it was. The room couldn't be pitch black, not with the light sneaking around the edges of the blinds and under the door, but Officer Al waved his light over the walls, starting from ceiling level. Black holes sucked out the light. Spots concentrated into pools at head level, returning to spots at lower levels and fading towards the floor.

"Conclusive," said Johnny as he turned the overhead lights on at Officer Al's request.

Now that we knew what to look for, we could see dark spots in the faux finish that might not be paint.

"Is there enough blood to run a DNA test?" I asked as we spilled back into the gallery to tell Mrs. Ly.

Officer Al's face warred between triumph and worry. "I think so, and of course we might find more when we do a formal crime scene search. But unless the victim is already in a database, either law enforcement or one of the commercial ones, it will hard to build a case when we don't have a body."

Johnny cleared his throat. "Maybe you do. The Justice of the Peace showed us a photo of the man found at a construction site, the one who worked on this house. Matt Davies' partner."

"Yes. Chris Herald." Officer Al nodded.

Mrs. Ly added, "Elisa's husband. Elisa was taken to the hospital earlier."

Officer Al sighed and looked down at Cupcake, once more seated, one ear up, by the bathroom door. "If he wasn't cremated, we might be able to get him exhumed, but first I've got to—"

"Pay your partner," I finished as he and Cupcake went out the back door.

The crowd had thinned down to just our relatives. As they gathered their belongings, Dianne's little cousin threw herself into our midst. "Lupita, Lupita, I took lots of pictures but I don't know how to send them to the cloud, like everybody else is doing."

"I'll have to do that. Why don't you take one more photo of me and my partners," said Dianne, selfie-smile at the ready as she put an arm around Johnny and me. "Now let's see—oh, *chica*, I do not want my hips all over Twitter. You aim up, and we'll lean down."

I flipped the tails of Dianne's glittery red scarf to the front to avoid displaying other body parts on Twitter, and we grinned like the air was full of nitrous oxide. Don't I wish.

"That's much better," said Dianne as she reclaimed her camera and scrolled back through her cousin's work. "Thank you, Mariposa. You've been a big help today."

Mariposa took off, her shoes slapping the wooden floor, reverberating to the rounded ceiling. "*Mamí*, Lupita says I've been a big help!"

"How many years until 'Do I hafta?'" I wondered aloud.

"We now have a complete set of photos of the party, all at three feet off the ground. *Madre de Dios*!" exclaimed Dianne.

Johnny and I squinted at the tiny viewer. Naturally, he caught on first.

"Someone's placing a plate of brownies on the special diets table. It has all the same markings as the one Mrs. Herald ate from, like the crumpled tape torn from another plate. Officer, look at this photo. Here's proof that someone put out food that would poison her."

Officer Al, returning from Cupcake's playtime/paycheck, took the camera and peered at the tiny rendering.

"It's timestamped and everything," said Dianne.

"But it's just an arm," he objected. "And even if you could find the person who wore a red plaid shirt—"

"Of course we can," said Johnny. "Our crew took many photos today."

PRISONER

*B*oots tramping down the gallery hall cut off Johnny's next statement. We all looked around and stepped closer together, suddenly on edge about the subject matter. As I'd noticed all afternoon, sound and words carried well in the vault-like hall. I didn't see any guests, but the elves giggled and gossiped from their original stations: the kitchen, the Christmas tree, the stairs. "Can you believe?" "Did you see the kittens? So sweet!" "Did you ever?" Their families grouped around them with their own murmurings.

Matt Davies gave us curt nods as he marched up to Johnny's grandmother. "Mrs. Ly, I've done all I can. I'll take the discounted amount, but I have to leave now. That—" He swallowed an epithet, probably racist, and glared at Dianne. "—young lady's uncle checked all these things on the list and says he'll be here with his crew next week to finish up."

"Very well." Mrs. Ly fished for her purse in her walker pocket.

We all looked back down at the camera viewer. The Black Orchids grabbed each other's arms, and the policeman squinted harder. Matt wore a red plaid shirt, just like the arm in Mariposa's photo.

"Okay, now I can ask questions about the brownies," whispered Officer Al as Johnny pulled us further down the hall, away from the paycheck drama. "But that doesn't get us any closer to solving the bathroom crime. There's still no body and a high likelihood of no identification."

Soft and slow, Johnny whispered as he handed over the brownie evidence, "Maybe there is. Chris Herald was dead when he hit the ground."

Officer Al looked puzzled. "The report said he was killed by the fall."

Johnny shook his head. "I saw the photos the JP took. There would have been blood everywhere if he'd struck his head."

"See Exhibit A, the bathroom," I added.

Johnny continued, "There was no blood in those photos. And if he had a medical event, like a heart attack, that would have shown up in the most cursory postmortem. First I'd see if the DNA from the blood in the bathroom matches Chris Herald's. I don't want to think it, but maybe Chris was killed here and taken to the construction site."

A choking noise made us all turn. Matt Davies had gone white under his blistered red skin. He couldn't get words out, and he ignored the check Mrs. Ly extended to him. The acoustics in this house were much too good.

"Mr. Davies, before you leave town, I need for you to come to the police station to answer some questions," said Officer Al.

Those magic words inspired the contractor. He spun around and ran.

Mrs. Ly shoved her rolling walker in his path, making him stumble. At the same time, Officer Al said a word in a language I didn't know. Cupcake launched onto Matt's back, and he stumbled down the porch steps and crashed on the ground. Heading for the porch, the officer spoke into his phone. I couldn't hear what he said over the screaming in the yard. We followed, after returning Mrs. Ly's walker to her.

"Get her off me! She's killing me!" howled Matt.

He tried to shove her off as she gnawed his arms and then his legs when he tried to crawl away. Delighted with her current job, she bit anywhere she could reach. Soon he was drenched in blood. Johnny went back into the house. I assume he was getting his first aid kit.

Officer Al gave another command to Cupcake. She let go and sat still, alert and expectant, as he snapped cuffs on Matt's legs. Behind us, Chantal's crew cheered, having abandoned their posts. A police car pulled up to the curb.

Mrs. Ly called, "My grandson can treat his wounds."

"We'll treat him at the station," said Officer Al. He waited until the police car drove away with the suspect and then waved Cupcake's snake. After the allotted amount of time, they rejoined us in the house. He said, "They don't like me to bring her to the station. Can she stay here?" After a nod from Johnny, he told Cupcake. "You stay with Johnny, Dianne, and JD now, you hear? You do what they tell you."

He pointed to each of us, as we collapsed in a row on the gold sofa. He transferred the plush snake with great ceremony to Johnny, who dangled it in front of her. She snatched it and started a tug of war.

To a chorus of relieved sighs, I asked Mrs. Ly, settling back into her chair, "What do you do after the open house?"

Mrs. Ly shook with laughter. "We repair to Casa Gracias in downtown Beauchamp to recover, despite all the food that's here."

"Beauchamp has a downtown?"

"A whole two blocks, possibly three, if you count the police station."

As though on cue, the elvish brigade and their families tromped through. My sisters flipped me a wave—I'm sticking to "wave"—and said it was the most exciting party they'd ever been to. I wasn't sure that was a compliment. They each had a grandparent by the arm. I plowed through the crowd to hug them. Grandmother said I played beautifully, and she looked forward to talking to me at Casa Gracias. Grandfather shook my hand with a firm message that I couldn't interpret. I was too frazzled. At least he didn't seem to hate me.

Dianne's mother, ever the event planner, was last in the parade.

Turning on my best smile, I leaned in to whisper in her ear. Then, with caterwauled directions to the restaurant (three blocks away), thank-yous, and see-you-soons dying down as the front door closed, I flopped back on the sofa between Johnny and Dianne.

With some major side eye, she asked, "What did you tell my mother?"

I shrugged. "Standard greetings. Hadn't had a chance to talk to her, the way parties are, especially for event planners, even those not on duty."

"JD, what did you tell my mother?" Her eyebrows and mouth turned into parallel lines as she accented each word.

"Okay, I told her I was so sorry I couldn't marry you, that's just how things go, but that I'd always love you as my dearest friend."

She gasped. "JD, you totally told her you were gay."

"Note that I did not actually say that. In case it comes up at my fictional wedding."

"She'll believe you're gay until your wedding—not at all fictional, just futuristic—and maybe beyond." Dianne, this time with no hesitation whatsoever, threw herself in my arms sideways on the couch. I too responded with no hesitation whatsoever.

At that point, Johnny's sister emerged, yawning, from Mrs. Ly's downstairs bedroom. When Cupcake glanced at her, Johnny snatched back the snake and hung it on his belt. Cupcake sighed and lay down with her chin on her front paws.

"So is this thing, like, over with?" Sophie Thi stiffened when she saw Johnny.

Mrs. Ly struggled to her feet. "You may drive me to Casa Gracias, Sophie Thi." Her gaze held a silent command.

Sophie Thi trembled under it, but she rallied the courage to say, "Grandmother says I have to apologize, Johnny."

"Not at all," he said. "I hope you are quite recovered."

Sophie Thi looked down and traced the floor with her black patent leather ankle boots. "When we were little? That rabbit? I thought you killed it. That lady on the floor brought it all back." She sighed down to her toes. "Grandmother said you were trying to save it from that big dog."

Johnny's voice dwindled to child level. "The dog from across the street had a rabbit in his mouth. I tried to make him drop it, and he bit me. The rabbit was already dead. I couldn't save it." He rolled up the left sleeves of his lab coat and shirt to expose some faded scars. "Grandmother took me to the hospital for stitches."

His grandmother spoke over his sob. "You were seven, John Ky, and there wasn't anything anyone could do. Sophie Thi, you were four. You didn't understand then, but twenty years later, it's time you did."

The old house creaked a solo in the silence.

His throat constricted, Johnny said, "I hope your holiday celebrations are merry, if I do not see you."

Sophie Thi folded her arms across her chest and said with a catch in her voice, "I couldn't stand a Christmas blow-out like Grandfather always put on, but Grandmother says nobody can, so you're going to do a traditional Jewish Christmas."

"Yes, dim sum in Austin's Chinatown," replied Johnny.

"Well—I might come then. And I'm sorry for, like, hating you." Helpless to wipe the years away, she shrugged and spread her hands wide.

"I'm sure I gave you ample cause. I have it on good authority that I was a strange child and possibly have not outgrown the tendency. I will be happy to see you at Uncle Phan's on Christmas," said Johnny, still grieving the rabbit, unable to return to the present day.

Mrs. Ly leaned her head against the red velvet and commanded, "Get my bag and sweater from the bedroom, Sophie Thi."

As Sophie Thi shuffled away, Mrs. Ly took her phone from a pocket on her walker and spoke a few low-pitched words, which I didn't hear because on the sofa we were slapping each other's shoulders in triumph for surviving the day.

Then as one, we stood, Johnny shedding his lab coat with its festive sprig of holly. I took it to throw into my office, and Dianne headed out to grab whatever she needed for the evening.

Cupcake jumped to her feet and growled.

FREEDOM

"**G**ood doggy," said Johnny, taking one slow step forward—quickly retracted when Cupcake showed her teeth and flared her ruff.

"Stupid dog! Let us go!" shouted Dianne as she stamped her foot.

Without rancor Cupcake braced herself in guard position.

"Let's all move in unison," I suggested. "She can't bite more than one of us at a time."

"Are you volunteering?" demanded Dianne. "Because I'm directly in front of her, and I don't volunteer."

"Did you see how many times she bit Matt in a minute? Let's sit down," suggested Johnny.

"Maybe we can get out the back door," said Dianne. She looked into Cupcake's eyes and sank back down on the sofa beside me.

"Were you on the track team?" asked Johnny. "A husky can run thirty miles per hour. And what about my grandmother?"

"Oh, I'm not moving," said the elderly lady, the lines around her eyes crinkling with amusement. "Besides, I have a black belt in walker weaponry. You wouldn't believe what people try to do to little old ladies. Usually just once per person, though."

Cupcake lay down by the front door with her tongue hanging out, laughing at us.

"Do you have any more dog treats?" whispered Dianne.

"In the clinic," said Johnny. He stood up and edged in that direction. So did Cupcake, with a menacing snarl. Johnny returned to his seat.

I pulled my phone out in slo-mo, in case Cupcake objected, and called everyone at Casa Gracias. Only Cherry picked up, but it was hard to get my point across through the party noise, which included a mariachi band. When she did understand, it was hard to communicate over her hysterical laughter. But after a few minutes, I could tell my partners, "They're sending someone to the police department to tell Officer Al. It's across the street from the restaurant."

Johnny leaned back and closed his eyes. "I'm glad for the excuse to stay here a minute. The best part of the day is the silence."

We didn't argue, though after a long minute Dianne said, "If you don't mind, Mrs. Ly, I think we should have the house blessing with the priest, the rabbi, and anybody else Johnny wants."

She waved her hand in a benediction.

"I agree," I said. "Maybe invite the widow Elisa and make it something to honor her husband."

"A very good idea," Johnny agreed, not opening his eyes. "Maybe the whole interfaith council would take part."

Footsteps smacked on the porch. The doorbell rang.

"Come in," I called to Officer Al's silhouette on the frosted glass door panel. "We can't come any closer."

He tried not to laugh, but chuckles escaped the side of his mouth as he patted her head. "Good girl, Cupcake! She didn't understand. She thought I meant for her to guard you. I'll take her with me. The weather's cool enough for her to wait in the car. Yes, girl, we'll play with the snake." Johnny tossed him the snake, and he threw it out the door into the yard. She fetched it, and they played tug of war on the porch.

"Did you learn anything from Matt?" I called.

Officer Al tried for a poker face. "I can't tell you anything about the case."

"Not even to the Assistant Justice of the Peace?" asked Johnny.

The conflict of duties turned Officer Al a bright tomato hue. "Well, I—No. Just no."

Dianne sighed. "Matt won't make his flight now. Too bad about his grandfather in Mexico."

"Mexico? He had a ticket for Canada," said the policeman.

"Ha! I knew it! He told us he was going to Mexico to see his grandfather. I knew he wasn't Mexican." Dianne's eyes gleamed in triumph.

I thought for a moment. "Johnny, when Chris said he wanted to meet Dianne, you weren't hanging up her photos, were you?" I gestured to the wall of history, where your (or at least my) eyes gravitated to the lovely Latina in her fluffy *quinceañera* and *folklórico* dresses. And the slinky formal she wore to the Great Waltz—I took a breath to focus on my current speech. "He hadn't seen her?"

Johnny's eyes glazed as he went into playback mode. "No, we were just talking. The walls were bare. I described our specialties and told him what CFE meant, Certified Fraud Examiner. He said, 'I'll come by on Monday to meet her. I might have some business for her and maybe the lawyer.' That's it, JD! He wanted Dianne to look at his business books, to see if he was being cheated. Somehow he let it slip to Matt, and Matt brained him with a tool that's probably still in his toolbox. Then Matt took Chris' body to the construction site. He poured bleach all over the bathroom trying to clean it up, not that it fooled the clever dog, and today he put a plate of peanut butter brownies where Chris' widow Elisa would find them, to make sure she couldn't look into the books either!"

"It's like you were there!" exclaimed the police officer.

"At the murder or the police station?" I asked.

It was interesting to see him turn even redder. There had to be an explosion point.

"And that murderer killed my first client!" Dianne tore off into a string of Hatch-pepper hot Spanish before she remembered that at least Officer Al could understand every word. He looked startled. I could make out every other word, and they were blistering.

"You'll have other clients," said Johnny, baffled. "We gave out all those coupons."

"I did not earn two degrees and two professional certifications to fill out standard 1040s for the whole town for free!" Dianne's voice rose into the Danger Zone. "I want to use those skills I went into life-long debt to acquire."

"Sometimes the police department contracts specialists," said Officer Al, looking doubtful. "Maybe even for this case. I'll take your card with me. And the coupon."

As Johnny's sister came out of the bedroom, arms full, Mrs. Ly said, "Or perhaps Elisa will want you to complete the audit her husband intended. The hospital says she's recovering nicely. You saved her life, John Ky. Sophie Thi, please drive me to Casa Gracias."

Dianne managed a thank you through her fuming while Johnny's grin spread from ear to ear. I clapped him on the shoulder in congratulations.

Still struggling, his sister managed to say through a scowl, "The house looks nice, all fixed up and everything. I just, I just don't want Grandma to abandon Beauchamp. It was always our escape, coming here."

Mrs. Ly patted her arm. "I'm not abandoning Beauchamp. I'm leaving it to my grandson, who, last I heard, is now Assistant Justice of the Peace, Assistant Animal Control Officer, the town's first cat veterinarian, head of the overflow animal shelter, and contributor to the Beauchamp All-Vegetable Orchestra."

"And musician. I'm going to play the gourd-olin," added Johnny. "Sophie Thi, you are welcome here any time."

His grandmother's face puckered into a grin, revealing the ghost of young Debbie Schwarz on her way to save Vietnam. "Possibly he is my revenge on the town. We shall see. Someday, Sophie Thi—all you young people—you'll wake up and realize you don't want to do what you've been doing anymore. And you'll stop doing it. Or leave."

Dianne and I locked gazes. That's why we were here.

Mrs. Ly pinched Johnny's cheek in that horrible, affectionate way some grandparents have. I flinched in sympathy.

She gave me one last look. "Send me a bill for your services today. If you're really interested in immigration—"

I started. "How did you know that?"

Her black eyes twinkled. "I know most everything that's said in this town, certainly what's said in the same room. I thought that would change when I retired as the school nurse, but somehow it hasn't. Anyway, close to half the population of this town was born in another country, so you might find yourself busier than you expected. I'll put you in touch with some organizations that would pay you to defend their clients."

She clumped toward the door as I gobbled my thanks. Officer Al and Cupcake followed her. Cupcake grinned at me, I swear.

Dianne sighed. "If you guys are going to do charity work, I'd better write some grants so we can keep the lights on, the seeds planted, and the clowder of cats fed."

I started to retort that come tax season, she'd be doing taxes for free at the library and senior center, just like she always did (while complaining about keeping her family's books and doing their taxes since she was fifteen), but then someone else leaned on the doorbell.

I blinked when I saw my grandfather on the porch.

"I hoped to see you in the restaurant, but as near as I could understand your sisters, a guard dog trapped you in the house. That one?" Grandfather struggled not to laugh as he looked over his shoulder at Cupcake on her way to Officer Al's car. She looked back, her head cocked to one side, her blue eyes aimed in different directions, one ear flopping forward, the other backward.

"Yeah, her." I glowered at the beast. Her panting sounded like laughter.

I stepped back so that Grandfather could come inside, but he shook his head.

"I'm driving back to Waco while it's still light, but I wanted to get a word in with you, difficult on these occasions. This one seemed memorable, which might be called successful."

"I think we beat out the Catholic church and their Living Nativity," I agreed.

"I heard about that. A murder investigation, an attempted murder, and the snake death should stick in people's minds for months." He did his best to still his shaking shoulders. "I brought you something for your new office, if you want it. It would go well with its traditional decor." He handed me a small oblong package.

I unwrapped it to find a foot-long mahogany pyramid with a brass name plate. It read "James Thompson, Attorney at Law" amid spots of tarnish. Time had rounded and splintered the wooden corners. It still smelled of lemon polish.

"This has to be Great-grandfather's!" I exclaimed, maybe squeaked. "Before he became a judge?"

"Yes, the first Attorney James Thompson. I used it after he retired, but I haven't wanted to hand it off to a younger generation, until now."

I gulped. "Thank you? I mean, yes, thank you. I'm happy to have it. Come see."

He followed me the few steps to my office, where I set the name plate on Mrs. Ly's massive old desk so that people would see it when they stepped through the doorway.

Looking around in approval, Grandfather said, "I think James Thompson the First would be proud of you, as am I. No matter what your father says." He turned to leave but paused with his hand on the front doorknob and looked at me with the wide-eyed Thompson baby blues. "By the way, we didn't hear from you about Christmas. You must have been too busy getting ready for this occasion to respond to anyone's messages."

My face felt hot as I accepted his excuse.

"Your father agreed to Christmas at our place in Waco. With the twins at university nearby, he's the only one left in Houston, and I didn't think you had any reason to go back there." As we left my office, his gaze fell on the reception desk with its orchids. "Memorable name you chose for your umbrella group. Everyone was talking about it. Symbolic, I understand."

Johnny glanced our way and volunteered, "Black orchids have many auspicious meanings, such as good fortune, success, strength."

"Very symbolic," I mumbled before he could say "virility" and "fertility."

"Excellent choice then." Grandfather smiled at all of us before departing.

I waved to Grandmother in the car before shutting the door.

Silence fell over the house, in its way just as magnified as the earlier sounds. In the hush, I expected an officiant to announce a prayer, a hymn, or a reading, with the congregation responding however they do these days—"Amen!" "Cool beans!" "Yo, man!"—whatever.

I sagged between and against the others. No one had the will or energy to report to Casa Gracias. I started when Chantal appeared in front of us. I should have heard the beat of her omnipresent high heels, but she held them in her hand. Even Chantal has limits. Good to know.

"Perfect end to a perfect party," she murmured as she waved her phone in the air for one last photo. "This looks like movie night at Casa Cortez."

Dianne laid her head on my shoulder. "Except no movie."

Chantal fiddled with her glucometer and smiled when it beeped. "I put away all the food. The elves can deep clean tomorrow. Now I'm gonna have me a taco, with half the shell even. You know what? You guys should make black orchid ornaments for your tree next year. Everyone loved JD's black orchid plant. No one ever saw anything like it before."

I covered my face.

"But it's not real," said Johnny.

"What do you mean?" asked Dianne. "It's real. I poked its roots before I watered it. I just hope we can keep it alive."

"That's not what I meant," Johnny argued, certain of himself. "I scraped one of the flowers, on the back, where it wouldn't show—"

Busted. I interrupted to confess first, "It's a real plant. It's just not really black. All the Austin florists said I should go to this orchid nursery over on Koenig. I told the lady there I had to have a live black orchid, and she snorted and said I didn't have the money, even if she had one. Then she took the darkest purple one and spray-painted the blooms black."

The silence was unbearable.

Then three pairs of arms circled me at various levels and hugged me so hard that I began to think this deal might work.

PART II
THE WAY OLD FRIENDS DO

A DAY IN THE LIFE

$\mathcal{I}$ must have missed that day in law school when they told us we'd have to pass judgment on dead bodies. I felt up to the challenge, though, since I was looking at human-sized bones scattered by construction equipment in a new subdivision. The axe-sized hole in the skull was a big clue about the cause of death.

It's true that since quitting my job at the high-powered Austin law firm and opening a private practice in Beauchamp, Texas (pronounced Beechem, no lie, population 7200, twenty-two miles east and south of Austin), I never know what the day will bring, but this was the first time I took on the mantle of Assistant to the Assistant Justice of the Peace. Kevin, the Alvarez County Justice of the Peace, is also the manager of the Beauchamp Sonic Drive-In, because requirements for this elected position in Texas are minimal (over age eighteen, county resident for six months). In little towns that don't have a medical examiner, the JP declares people dead and why. Some JPs rely on law enforcement to tell them, but Kevin's faith was shaken after the sheriff told him that a body with two bullet holes from the same gun was a suicide. My partner Johnny Ly volunteered as Kevin's assistant in charge of deaths, leaving Kevin to preside over the small claims court and weddings that he prefers. Johnny's a vet, but he's had more forensic training than the standard two-weeks Texas offers its JPs. Sometimes I think I should run for that office, so I can be JD Thompson, JD, JP. It has a certain ring.

I was subbing for Johnny this morning because he's Beauchamp's Assistant Animal Control Officer too, and ten days ago, he went out to deal with a wild hog in the city limits. The police brought him home —Johnny, not the hog—with bruises and broken bones from excessive hog brutality.

Johnny, a vegetarian since I first met him as my freshman roommate, now crunches bacon every day as revenge.

The rumble of the arriving sheriff's car inspired me to wind up my service as Assistant Assistant JP. I didn't want to argue about whether an axe wound in the head indicated suicide. I snapped photos of the bones and sent them to Johnny for his medical opinion—no way did I want to end up in court explaining my qualifications. Kevin, who always comes out on these calls while avoiding the corpse, gave me a stack of Sonic coupons in gratitude.

I wasn't in the mood for a Sonic burger. I went to one of Beauchamp's ten taco trucks instead. I photographed my order to put on Twitter because I'm in charge of social media, being as I suck at it less than my partners. That's how things usually go with us: Johnny and Dianne are experts in their fields, and I cover everything else. Isn't that what friends are for?

A text came in from Dianne as I was getting back in my car:

Miss Leigh's not answering her phone. Please check.

Law school didn't cover that kind of work either, but that's also what friends are for.

I'd better start closer to the beginning. Six months ago, I received an email from my college roommate Johnny. After speedily earning a BS, DVM, and veterinary acupuncture degrees, he crashed and burned out of zoo vet school. His grandmother was moving into an assisted-living community and wanted to turn her historical home over to him. Rising like a castle from the rubble of a little Texas town that nobody ever knew about, much less remembered, Gregg House was big enough to house his feline veterinary practice and several other professional offices downstairs, with plenty of living space upstairs. Would his former housemates like to join him?

Between ten and twenty people qualified under that term. In the summer before sophomore year, my ex Dianne Cortez rented a large old house near the university and invited her friends to live with her, somehow including Johnny and me. We, she, and Chantal Gaumont stayed in Casa Cortez for the rest of our education; others came and went. Now all those others were settled into homes and career paths elsewhere, except Chantal, who didn't think she could build a singing career from Beauchamp. But my heart leapt for joy at the thought of swerving off the highway to success. Dianne dragged me to a brutalist restaurant, all gray with sharp angles, to explain with damning spreadsheets and buzz-killing charts why this was the stupidest idea ever.

As she said, "It's completely impractical, even in a best-case scenario," we locked gazes, hers as passionate as Dianne always is when explaining her beloved numbers. Then hell froze over, the Cubs won the Series—wait, they did—and somewhere a lion and lamb lay down together, both standing up again after a shared cigarette. A tear welled in one beautiful brown or possibly hazel eye and left a track through Dianne's perfect makeup.

"I'm going to do it," she whispered. Then she dragged me to this new salsa dive she'd discovered, because dancing is Dianne's response to everything in life.

Now a big fake bronze sign in front of Gregg House announces this splendid edifice to be the home of Black Orchid Enterprises, followed by, in smaller letters, the names of the principals in alphabetical order.

The next line says *Se habla español* and characters that Johnny says mean "Vietnamese Spoken Here." The last person who would have needed that was Johnny's grandfather, some years deceased. Johnny says it shows inclusiveness. Given our location, I'm not sure that's a virtue, but Johnny keeps saying something about being the change you want to see in the world. He also thinks that with our combination of skills, we could do detective work, not as stupid as it sounds: his expertise with patterns makes him a great diagnostician; Dianne, a Certified Fraud Examiner, does the same thing with numbers and money; and my law skills should be good for something, if only saying, "That's illegal, guys." I suggested we establish ourselves individually first.

We do have clients, mostly people using the free consultation coupons we handed out at our Christmas open house and grand opening (well pet exams from Johnny, basic tax returns from Dianne, twenty-minute legal consultations from me). I've explained to many people that the Stand Your Ground law does not mean shooting somebody you don't like and claiming you were scared, I've filled out simple wills, and I almost got through a mediated divorce in the free twenty minutes. However, though the couple brought a list of their proposed property division, at the last minute the wife said that he was welcome to the second refrigerator, like they agreed, but her father had put the fittings on the ice maker, and it was just wrong for her husband to have those when her father, with his very own hands, installed them. Things went south from there, and they left before the billable hours started.

That's why I agreed to take on this eldercare gig, or babysitting old ladies, even though it makes me feel as slimy as my cousin Jeff, who works for one of those debt-collecting law firms. Johnny pointed out that robbing the elderly wasn't a job requirement, that we could fulfill our duties with honesty and compassion. I brought up liability, and Dianne said that's why I'd write a contract. She too wanted that steady paycheck.

And I like Leigh Brandon. She was the first to welcome us to the town. She tottered across the street, dressed all in blue, even a blue tinge to her white hair, coaxed into a puffy page boy. She was the widow of a Texas oilman, for all that she bought her clothes on sale at Target. She brought us a little box of chocolates as a treat for our moving ordeal, just like neighbors used to do before I was born, so I'm told. Maybe not exactly, though.

Johnny served us tea, and we all took a bite of chocolate, as all our mothers from separate cultures taught us. Johnny rolled it on his tongue and approved with a slow smile. "My favorite flavor."

Dianne's polite smile gave way to obvious contemplation of the age-old dilemma: spit or swallow. Her gaze darted from me to Johnny, now on his second chocolate.

Thus warned, I took one bite, as you must, and set the rest on the napkin. Somebody had to stay sober.

Miss Leigh said in lyrical Southern accents, "I've known your grandmother ever since she moved to Beauchamp, Johnny, though we were out on the farm then. I promised her I'd look after you. She says you're inclined to be nervous, and I brought you some of Claire's chocolates—my daughter Claire, you know. She runs the cutest little bakery in Colorado."

Johnny, the only one who could manage it, thanked her with grace and genuine gratitude. I keep telling my friends I have to have plausible deniability if they want me to defend them in court. Translated, that means don't commit crimes right in front of me, like eating cannabis-infused chocolates. He put them out of my sight after she left, and I didn't see any more, not until she brought over casseroles after Johnny's accident, along with several boxes of chocolates.

Miss Leigh's two out-of-state daughters visited us during their annual Christmas visit. They wanted to hire somebody close by for emergencies, to make day-to-day decisions, and to ward off predatory grifters. Miss Leigh agreed to the plan, as long as we understood that we were *her* employees. Dianne had the daughters funnel money into a local credit union account that she could monitor and make sure bills were paid, house and lawn maintained. They were, Miss Leigh still being as sharp as Johnny's vaccination needles, and today was the first day we had to do anything like a welfare check.

I knocked on the front door of our only steady income, the trim ice-blue frame house perched across the street to the south from Gregg House. After minutes of silence, I pounded, even louder, and then one last time, while shouting, "Miss Leigh! Miss Leigh, please open the door." Like many trusting souls, she had a hiding place for her house key, which I won't reveal, but I retrieved it, rather than go across the street for the one she gave us.

The house was dark and unoccupied. It was neat, tidy, everything in its place. The refrigerator held nothing that would spoil quickly. I crossed the street to report.

Stepping into Gregg House's massive gallery-hallway, with its ceiling tall enough to have its own weather, is like entering another century. Despite efforts at upkeep that included warm red-brown wood paneling and matching floors, Johnny's grandmother's grandparents' furniture, fine examples from the early twentieth century, still keep the antique vibe of warm gold and red. The only twenty-first century intrusions are (1) a TV with a door-sized screen, covered by a Vietnamese silk painting of two stylized Siamese cats on a yellow and gold background, and (2) an uber-recliner, bought for Johnny, just after his hog encounter.

He was, of course, reading his tablet in his gold recliner, its back to the TV because that's what Johnny thinks of TV. I handed him tacos and the one beer he drinks at lunch while we waited for Dianne to get off her phone. Lounging on the gold sofa, she was flipping between Spanish and English, which is hard for me to follow. Bandages on her hands and arms made me glad that I'd drawn Justice of the Peace duty instead of holder-of-cats for Johnny's morning appointments. She still looked gorgeous, but I've never seen her any other way. Her blacker-than-black hair framed her oval face, glowing in its warm terra cotta hue. She hadn't bothered to capture the hair in a professional bun, and it trailed around her shoulders, somehow managing an illicit appeal.

Finally she hung up. She popped the top on a can of some kind of sugar-free Pepsi, her drink of choice since high school.

I gave my report and said to her, "This is where you do that thing called explaining."

LOST!

*D*ianne took a deep breath, preparing for a long story. "I had a quick lunch with Gabriel from the credit union. You can have my tacos. Gabriel asked if I'd seen Miss Leigh lately, hinting that I should. I just checked her account, and she took out a big chunk of money last week, right after our monthly meeting. And yesterday she basically cashed out the account, in person. She told Gabriel it was for a van for her daughter Maureen; she was driving it to Maureen's house in Mississippi to surprise her." Dianne took another swig of Pepsi. "Gabriel felt queefy about a seventy-year-old lady driving herself to Mississippi with enough money to ransom a small child or a big dog. He felt better when he walked her out to the car, a big honking Pacifica, and saw a young guy driving. He thought there were people in the back seats too. He watched them drive to the gas station next to the credit union, and the kid pumped the gas. Probably paid cash, because he went into the store first. He looked like a teenager, with light brown skin, short curly black hair.

I asked, "What's the problem? She's going to see her daughter. She hired somebody to drive her."

"Except that they headed west on the highway, not east. And why does she need cash when she has these modern financial tools like checks and credit cards, which she has no objection to using? Why didn't she tell us she was leaving? She knows we're responsible for her safety."

"To a limited extent, carefully specified in the contract."

Johnny kept staring at his tablet. A kitten slept on his shoulder. Johnny's plan for a no-kill town seems to be taking in all the unwanted area cats and kittens. "Probably a good explanation for everything."

Dianne's eyes met my mine. Johnny, ignoring a puzzle?

"What are you reading?" I asked, super casual.

"*Emma*, by Jane Austen. It comes highly recommended, but I'm not sure how interesting the problems of rich girls can be."

Dianne's eyes went wide. She mouthed, "*Johnny's reading fiction.*"

Terminally curious, Johnny on any given day is reading at least three books, maybe economics, medical, historical, physics, public policy, culture, or (recently) vegetable gardening. He reads fiction when he's given up, a retreat from the once-fascinating world.

"So," I said, trying to needle Johnny into engagement. "Miss Leigh's one of your grandmother's friends, and Gabriel said the van was heading west yesterday. Maybe they went to Austin to see her." When he didn't look up, I added, "Are you calling or shall I?"

With a noise that sounded like "Pfui," Johnny pulled out his phone and tapped. When he put the phone on speaker, we could all hear the immediate voicemail message.

Dianne said, "Miss Leigh's in that group, Promise of a New Day, that your grandmother founded."

Promise of a New Day, a community improvement group, meets in Gregg House, as do the Boy Scouts, Beauchamp Library Board, Alvarez County Young Mothers, and Friends of Animals. We also rent out the meditation room for weddings. Ask us about renting the whole house! Mrs. Ly never wanted to, but we could be persuaded. Gotta pay those student loans somehow.

Dianne scrolled through her contacts and came up with the president's name. "Hello, may I speak to Mrs. Langston? She is? I was trying to get in touch with Mrs. Brandon, but she seems to be out of town too. They did? Thank you very much." Her expression tightened throughout the call. She frowned after her phone screen went dark. "Someone—a daughter, I think—says the two of them have gone to visit your grandmother in Austin."

Johnny tapped his phone again. The pain lines in his face deepened with each unanswered ring.

I wanted him engaged, not worried. "I'll run over to Austin and check on her. Probably nothing—but we can't have people disappearing." I was sure Mrs. Ly had stepped out to the store and forgotten her phone, or it lay uncharged in her purse, but Johnny didn't need any more worries.

In forty-five minutes, I was knocking on Mrs. Ly's door. In another ten minutes, I was knocking on her neighbors' door. An elderly man, white of skin and hair, bent with the insults of age, shuffled to the door. He said Mrs. Ly left yesterday morning around 10:30 in a new white van, the paper tag still in the back window. A slim young brown man helped with the luggage and then got into the driver's seat.

"Pretty light in the loafers," the old man observed.

Because I needed his help, I clenched my teeth and smiled around them.

Unaware, he continued, "She asked me to watch the place a few days because she was going back to Beauchamp to take care of her grandson who broke his foot or leg or something."

I didn't provide my expert knowledge on that subject, just thanked him and returned to my car. I sent a text to Johnny and Dianne before starting back home. Prompt or cowardly? You decide.

I arrived at Gregg House just as another elderly man navigated to the front door. He approached each of the steps as though it were Mt. Everest. He used to be tall, he used to have good hair, his eyes used to be a sparkling blue, and he'd hit a million golf balls on a thousand courses, leaving him faded, shuffling, and squinting, despite glasses and a cane. He introduced himself as Buddy Hamilton and reminded me he'd attended the last Promise of a New Day meeting. I hadn't; that night was Johnny's turn to moderate, chaperone, or whatever we do when crashing these meetings to keep an eye on the radicals using our house.

In the reception hall-gallery, I was surprised to find another meeting in progress, like a political phone bank, with Johnny, Dianne, and a woman I didn't know all making calls on their phones. The new woman was at least ten years older than me, but I wouldn't hold it against her. She was efficiency in action in her denim skirt and crisp blouse with little blue snowflake buttons, an outfit that screamed "teacher." No doubt when spring officially arrived, she'd change the button covers to flowers.

Between calls, Dianne introduced her as Sierra Schliemann, secretary of Promise of a New Day. Dianne invited her to bring her membership list and help identify Miss Leigh's other passengers.

Sierra gave me a distracted smile and said, "We can't account for Leigh Brandon and Doria Langston. And my mother, but she might be sleeping. I guess she's not feeling good, Buddy?"

She looked at the new arrival as Dianne ushered him to a yellow chair. Lowering himself into the chair required all his attention, but when he was settled, he answered with a slight smile. "I think she's feeling better. She left yesterday morning with some of her girlfriends to visit Debbie Ly in Austin. They plan to spend a few days doing girl stuff, for the last time, you know."

Johnny explained in a soft voice, "At the last Promise meeting, Sierra's mother Linda announced that her doctors were stopping her cancer treatments."

Dianne and I murmured incoherent condolences. Dianne whispered to me that Buddy had lived with Linda Schliemann for several years. She didn't know exactly why he invited himself today.

Sierra swallowed and responded just as incoherently before turning to Buddy. "Mother didn't say anything about going to Austin. Of course, I was in class all day, and then everyone had soccer after school. Maybe she told my sister or brother. Brothers." She twisted her lips upward in a heroic effort. "We all visited her after treatment stopped, and she told us to take a week off while she decided what to do, like maybe get into hospice. She said everybody needed a break after taking her to all her treatments. It used to get wild, with my brother, sister, and I comparing schedules to see who would take or pick up Mother for treatment. After Mrs. Ly moved to Austin, sometimes we took Mother there the night before, and she and Mrs. Ly would take one of those ride-hailing cars to the cancer center. Of course, now Mother's in a wheelchair. That must make it more difficult for her friends to take her places." Her face sagged, ready to weep. "I didn't know she'd go downhill that fast, in a wheelchair as soon as treatment stopped."

Buddy shook his head an eighth of an inch, like Johnny does now, marking himself as another unwilling member of the Chronic Pain Club. "She quit fighting after that last doctor visit. Oh, I could tell you stories. My wife, she struggled with cancer for years. It's hard."

Sierra winced and looked down.

"Did your mother have things she still wanted to do, last goals she wanted to achieve?" asked Johnny, so withdrawn into his recliner that I expected velour to sprout on his face.

Sierra frowned. "She's done most of it. The Promisers took her out to lunch the day after the last meeting. My sister China went with her and said Mother thought the worst thing would be missing the Mueller report, that she's followed every special counsel investigation since Watergate. China was shocked when her friends said she just ought to go to Washington and ask him herself, play the old dying white lady card. They joked about breaking into his office if he wouldn't talk to her."

"My grandmother's just as political, always wanting me to go protest something with her when I was in high school. And my parents made me go, and later my brother and sisters, to take care of her." Dianne shook her head. "Like she needed us! She said to fall on your right side to protect your liver if the police beat you and to write your contact info in Sharpie on the inside of your upper arm. That way someone can identify your body. And never, ever mess with federal property, because there's penalties for that. So I hope your mother's friends were joking."

In the silence that dropped like dead grackles from the sky, Buddy said, "She did want to spend more time with her son, the first one, the Black guy."

Sierra Schliemann looked up at Johnny's raised eyebrow and explained, "Mother married when she was in college. Her parents didn't like it because he was Black. He died in Vietnam soon after, before he even got to see his son. Mother became a teacher, and later she married my father. They had two more children after me, Micky and China. They run Dad's Chrysler dealership in Elrod. Dad wanted to adopt Shawn, my older brother, but his grandparents didn't want their son's name erased. He ended up spending most of his school time with them because the kids here were mean. That's how Mother and Debbie Ly became close friends, because Shawn's only friend was Mark Loc Ly, who is half-Vietnamese."

"My father," said Johnny.

Sierra glanced an apology at Johnny. "Beauchamp in the 70s was a lot more racist then."

I kept my eyebrows firmly in place and watched Dianne in a similar struggle. We hadn't noticed the progress.

"After Mother put us to bed at night, I'd hear her calling Shawn to ask about his homework and read him a bedtime story. We did know him because he spent a lot of weekends and most summers with us. He had some troubles when he was young, but a lot of young people do. He's doing really well now, a computer programmer in San Marcos." Her tone was that of one who really wanted to believe.

"A young Black man was driving the van," said Johnny.

"Shawn's over forty, and his only son is eight. Maybe it's Doria Langston's grandson. He drives her everywhere." She glanced at a new text on her phone. "China says Mrs. Brandon picked up a new white Chrysler Pacifica yesterday for Maureen, her eldest daughter."

Johnny stirred in his chair and entered the conversation. "I'd like to talk to your sister, Sierra."

She tapped her phone and handed it to him. He got two for the price of one: China and Micky were both on the video call.

He introduced himself as Miss Leigh's guardian and asked what they knew about the trip, which I now thought of as The Ride of the Septuagenarians.

"Nothing," Micky exploded. His face was red, working on an early stroke. "How can you call yourself a guardian when you let your charge escape like that? And she took my mother with her! My mother is seriously, terminally ill. I've a mind to sue you."

He and his two sisters looked a lot alike, as though a beginning live-drawing class tried to draw the same model. But whereas Sierra was pretty enough to make me overlook the ten years, and her younger sister cute enough not to need any overlooking, Micky Schliemann was a troll version.

"You can waste your money however you please, but your efforts might be better spent in ascertaining your mother's location and condition." Johnny didn't sound at all worried—which he shouldn't, because I drew up the contract. There was no way we were liable for our client's running away with her friends.

Little sister China, whose marital status was relevant to my interests, asked, "They left yesterday? Alone?"

"No, we have information that Doria Langston and possibly her grandson went as well. They picked up my grandmother in Austin at 10:30."

"Are you going to call the police? Set up one of those Silver Alerts?" asked China, worry lines creasing her pretty brow.

Johnny steepled his fingers together. "That would be up to you. Silver Alerts are intended for Alzheimer's patients and others who can't care for themselves. It looks to me like Mrs. Brandon and her friends are taking very good care of themselves. She bought a van, which she can well afford. She has other people with her, including a young driver. They chose not to tell their families, but that's not illegal."

"And Debbie Ly is a nurse," Sierra interjected. "Maybe she's helping Mother."

"That's just like you, Sierra, taking the side of those bleeding heart—"

"I'm not taking sides," she flared at her brother, in a voice guaranteed to quell ten-year-old hoodlums. "I think we should get a Silver Alert. I'm just saying that she's probably not in danger."

Their not-at-all stepfather spoke up. "Your mother's real good at taking care of herself. And if she wants to die on her dream vacation, well, why not? You see things differently when you get to be our age. I wouldn't worry about her."

"You're seven years older than Mother," said Micky over China's muttered, "I'm sure you won't."

Sierra started gathering her things. "I'll be right over."

Picking up the cue, Buddy started the struggle to get to his feet.

Johnny said in what he'd call valediction, "Members of our firm will be on the road shortly to try to intercept them. I agree with Sierra, in that I see little reason to worry, but we do want to confirm their health and well-being."

"What?" I said, echoed by Dianne an octave higher.

We ushered out our guests like Sierra Schliemann running a fire drill with her class of young monsters: firm and quick, but steady.

"Just exactly who are these members of the firm going on this pointless road trip?" I asked as I flopped onto the sofa.

Johnny got busy with his tablet as Dianne released the kitten brigade from their incarceration in Johnny's bedroom. "I think they went to Washington, DC. They'd already be in Vicksburg, if that were their destination. While you went to Austin, JD, we talked to Maureen, who says they didn't. We called the other daughter, Claire, and she hasn't seen or heard from her mother either. You two should go to DC after them."

I objected, "Even if you're right, there must be a million ways to get to DC."

Johnny held up his tablet to show us the map. "Actually, only two, though with variations. You either go north to Dallas, then east, and then north through Virginia. Or you could wind through Texas two-lane highways to the east, then through Louisiana, Mississippi right through Vicksburg, north through Alabama, and pick up the other route."

Dianne added, while stroking her favorite kitten, the little white one. "We're pretty sure they took the first one. I called my mother—you remember how she made friends with everybody at our open house?—and she said Doria Langston called her last weekend to ask if she knew someone in the Dallas area who could paint cars, for a friend who lived there. Of course *Mamí* told her about *Tío* Abejundio, her youngest brother, that *pendejo*. Then I called him, and he said they arrived yesterday afternoon. He gave their van a temporary, quick-drying paint job—it's now mint green—and sold them some stickers and signs they could use to change its appearance." Her face darkened. "And he showed the kid how to make new license signs, changing the numbers just enough. The ladies really don't want anybody tracking them."

"But we're going to?" I asked. "Have you thought—"

"Yes," said Dianne. "We can get to DC in less than 24 hours, if we don't stop except to trade drivers. Her daughter Claire told Johnny that Miss Leigh is inflexible about traveling: she stays in Ramada Inns. And her favorite restaurant is Kip's Big Boy, which turns into Shoney's as you go east. She loves the breakfast buffet, where she'll walk in and exclaim over all the choices and then choose a spoonful of scrambled eggs, one piece of bacon, a quarter piece of waffle, and a fruit cup. Every time. Failing Kip's, she leans towards diners and drive-ins, though she has enough money to stay in and eat at five-star places every night and every meal. Oh, and I called Chantal to come stay with Johnny. She was coming to help with taxes soon anyway; she can get started early."

"Chantal?" Johnny shrunk back into his chair.

Everyone agrees that Chantal Gaumont is going to be wildly successful, if she can just focus. She showed up at college with the rest of us after plowing through beauty school, so she'd always have a job to fall back on, in case the accounting major didn't work out, but what she really wanted to do was sing. She was always in the music building, taking lessons and practicing, or in bars, singing and learning how to mix drinks, to have something else to fall back on. Because she wanted to sing in a close harmony group, she recruited members from the house she shared with us, and MulticulturABBA—soon abbreviated to MultiABBA, because who can say that?—was born, all of us having grown up dancing to our parents' ABBA albums and all the subsequent ABBA tribute bands. She learned graphic arts and web design to do her own publicity. After college, she took up pole dancing, which is my fault. When grad school distracted the rest of us from our singing careers, I pointed out that her counterpart in the A-teens went on to be a pole dancer. Finally Chantal found something truly reliable that could provide rent money by the first. She now travels, sings, and (when necessary) pole dances. Living (or visiting) with her means continuous music, like singing four-part harmony over three floors.

We love her.

And she is just too much 24/7, especially for Johnny, who has been known, on his bad days, to start shaking when she enters the room.

I thought about it. On the one hand—road trip! On another, staying up all night for any purpose has lost its charm, particularly on a lost cause like this one, with so many unknowns that it seemed pointless. On yet another hand (or foot), if it were my grandmother, would I go, hopeless or not? I certainly would, even though my father would tell me to leave it to the police and the private detectives he would hire. On still another appendage, Miss Leigh was not my grandmother, just my client. Then again (now that I was approaching octopus-level), when one of Dianne's friends went missing in our sophomore year, didn't I jump up and join the search crew, though I didn't know her well and was well beyond trying to impress Dianne? I didn't want someone in our community to just disappear, with no one to care about her. "Okay," I said. "As long Chantal's going to be here."

We looked at Johnny.

He sighed. "Okay. Chantal it is."

"Fifteen minutes," said Dianne.

ROAD TRIP

By the time I packed and waved goodbye to Johnny, Dianne was loading a 24-can case of no-sugar Pepsi in my Hyundai Sonata, the obvious vehicle choice. I have to fold myself in two to ride in Dianne's Honda.

Maybe she wouldn't mourn the Jaguar's passing more than once an hour. My father paid its down payment when I passed the bar, and I sold it before I moved to Beauchamp, to the everlasting sorrow of my friends who always claimed to have minds above material possessions. It was a fun ride, even more fun if you didn't have to make the monthly payments.

"I thought you were down to one Pepsi per day," I said as I threw my gym bag in the trunk.

"Emergency," she snapped.

After we moved in at the end of last year, Dianne announced at the dinner table that she was giving up all her vices except for one sugar-free Pepsi per day. No more smoking, bars (except for dancing), gaming, social media, dieting, dating—"

I cleared my throat. "Dating is a vice?"

She drooped like a pansy in a Texas summer. "The way I do it must be. I'm so bad at it."

I looked at Johnny, whose glassy eyes told me he wasn't joining this party. I chose my words like they were priced by Neiman-Marcus. "Dianne, as your three-time ex, I say with confidence that you're not bad at dating."

She snapped her spine straight to glare at me. "Oh, yeah? Then why aren't we together, as my mother keeps asking me? And why can't I make a connection last even as long as ours?"

I let out a long breath, considering. I used my fork to push the eggplant lasagna around on my plate. Dianne and I know exactly why it doesn't work for us, but we fall back on "It's complicated" for everyone else. I rose and put my hands on her shoulders as I quoted from "When All Is Said and Done," the part about it being no one's fault.

She jumped up, knocking me backwards with her chair. "Effing ABBA is not the effing Bible," she shouted as she ran to the staircase.

After a door slammed upstairs, Johnny asked, "They aren't?"

So if Dianne was now diving off her wagon, I was not going to comment, not when I had to spend 25 hours in a car with her. I laid my suit bag over all the luggage, because there's nothing like a suit to claim your turf, particularly when you're a tall blond white dude (with a mysterious but invisible 6% Native American DNA). Dianne and Johnny call it "privilege wear." We might need it as we stormed the halls of government, or at least followed our client when she did.

I have to be exhausted to sleep in the car, which led me to say I'd drive first. "What odds do you give us? Catching up with the escapees, that is."

She frowned. "Pretty good, if we're right about where they're going."

"Oh?"

"Yes. The GPS instructions would be similar. Probably they'll take the fastest route, but they'll sleep at night, unlike us. They've got one driver. At their ages, they'll stop more often. Yes, we'll catch them up. You didn't ask if we'd recognize them when we passed them."

And I didn't. Ask, that is. We stopped by the Sonic Drive-In on our way out of town to spend my Justice of the Peace salary from the morning and charge my batteries with coffee.

Dianne canted her seat back as far as it would go, donned her ear plugs and lavender-scented eye mask, and set to falling sleep, which she can do in ten minutes. I was glad. I had a plan.

I didn't hear a word from her until Waco, as I was turning into Oakdale Assisted Living. I don't know how to spell the word she said as she regained consciousness.

She tried again. "Where are we?"

"Waco. We're going to see my grandfather."

"*Madre de Dios*, this isn't spring break, JD. We're racing the clock here."

"Thirty minutes, tops. We've got to do this."

"Why? I said we'd catch up to them, but that doesn't mean we have time to waste."

"It's important. Dreams are important."

"Am I supposed to understand that?"

"You do, or you wouldn't be filling out 1040s in Beauchamp, Texas."

Since I was driving, she couldn't stop me, though if complaints were bricks, she could have built the border wall from California to the Gulf of Mexico. She had enough respect for the elderly to shut up when I knocked on the door of my grandfather's cottage.

Former US Attorney Jimbo Thompson (one of a long line of Attorneys James Thompsons) raised his bushy white eyebrows almost to his thick white hair. It's a comfort to me that the Thompson men keep their hair, often described as leonine. I intend to grow a full mane.

"JD, such a surprise. The family is well?" His rumbling bass voice would blow out a speaker. I wish I could have heard him in court. "Arline, our grandson JD is here."

I don't know if Grandmother needed the reminder, but it gave me twinge of sorrow of the Skywalker NOOOOOOOOOOOOOOOOOOO variety. "You remember my partner Dianne Cortez?" I said to him and the tiny woman on the sofa.

Grandmother turned her gaze from the floor-to ceiling window across the back wall. "My, you've grown, JD. And your little friend too. How are you doing in school? Are you getting married soon?"

"JD's out of school, Arline. He's passed the bar," Her husband reminded her in a tender voice, which I was glad to hear. "Miss Cortez is his business partner."

I let the sarcastic tone to "business" slide. Dianne ignored it too as she sat on the couch and put her hands over her knees to hide a hole in her tights. In the distant past, she attended holiday dinners as The Girlfriend; she had a standard to maintain.

Grandmother said, cheery and unembarrassed, "That's right. He left his good job with a major law firm to set up practice with his kooky college roommates in a cow patty town in the middle of nowhere, and what he's thinking, I couldn't tell you. Completely trashing his career, that's what he's doing."

I spoke a bit louder to cover the choking sound Dianne made. "That's right, Grandmother. We were glad to see you at our open house. You'll have to come visit us in a few weeks to see the bluebonnets. We have plenty of room."

Grandfather fetched glasses of water to cover the awkwardness. "To what do we owe the honor?" he asked as he handed them to us.

"I'm here on behalf of a client." I enjoyed saying that. "You were a Marine in Vietnam, Hotel Company. A while back, you said that one of your fellow Marines undertook an important task in DC."

"Bobby Three Sticks, yes. Good man, in the Corps and out of it."

"My client wants to talk to him."

He set his glass down with care and growled, "Have you lost your mind?"

"I hope not. My client is taking a terminally ill friend to Washington, DC, because the friend's chief worry about dying is not knowing how the Mueller Report comes out. I was thinking you might call in a favor."

"And you think the Special Counsel, who's running the tightest, most leak-proof investigation ever, is going to tell his findings to a bunch of dot—nice old ladies?" He glanced an apology to Grandmother, who'd returned to watching birds on the bright winterberry outside the window. It's an odd tree, a holly that drops its leaves in the winter, leaving whitish branches covered with red berries.

"No, but he might have his staff say a few nice words. It might forestall their trying to break into his office. They don't have the skills for that—I think—and it could only go badly."

"You want me to blackmail him with that taradiddle?"

"No, I want you and he to show compassion for someone near death, who looks to him to save the country, whether or not that's true, the way we hope people will show mercy on us at that time."

"Now and at the hour of our death," Dianne murmured, maybe in prayer, but not likely from the woman who last attended Mass on Christmas Eve.

I thought the look she gave me was admiring, except that she pinched my arm and pointed to where a watch would be if she wore one.

Grandmother broke the turgid silence that followed by exclaiming, "Oh look! A cardinal! He matches the berries."

I said to my grandfather, "I guess I've asked for too many favors in the past."

"You never asked for anything! You wouldn't accept anything! You could have gone to my school back East. The family has enough contacts to get you into the best firms in the country—or judge's office, if you wanted to go that route—but you wanted to do things your way!" His explosion had the heft of years and unwilling restraint behind it.

I kept my voice level. I've had practice. "Yes. I wanted to see what I could do for myself. But I can't do this, and I want to, for my client's and her friends' sake. If you help me this time, I promise in the future to always ask for help when I need it, like my cousin Jeff."

Grandfather glowered while Grandmother recited: "It's a wonder that young man was ever toilet-trained. He expects us to do everything else for him."

Cousin Jeff was indeed a sore point. I knew by the time I was nine never to lend him money.

Grandfather shook his head. "I can contact Bobby, but you mustn't expect anything."

I stood up, in response to Dianne's tapping her wrist again. "I won't, but I appreciate the effort. I'll send you their names, though, in hopes."

Dianne shook my grandmother's hand. "So nice to see you both again, Mrs. Thompson."

"Yes indeed, dear. Are you going to make some music for us?"

That tugged my heart. Grandmother gave me my first piano lessons, came to all my recitals and band concerts after I took up the trombone in high school (because the prettiest girls were in the band), and encouraged me to practice when I visited her. She even attended some of MultiABBA's concerts. She used to say how much she loved the originals. Every generation has its ABBA. Mine was A-Teens, and the kids now have the *Mamma Mia* movies, but of course we work with the source material as much as possible.

I said, my voice higher and tighter than I liked, "You don't have a piano or a horn for me to play, Grandmother."

Dianne patted her hand. "We could sing for you."

If she broke into "Man After Midnight" or "Voulez-Vous," I was going to stomp her toes. Instead she started the song about Paris in the summer.

I let her finish the verse about strolling down the Champs Elysées eating croissants. When she came to my side and linked arms with me, I harmonized on the chorus. I gazed into her eyes as we sang about the memories of that summer. We had no accompaniment, only a third of the harmony, and a tempo some would call too slow, but the song actually made a nice torchy duet.

Grandfather joined his wife on the couch. She put her arm through his; he patted her knee with one hand.

When the last line died away, he said in a softer voice striated with multiple meanings, "Thank you."

"Yes. Me too." That's me, Captain Awkward.

Dianne and I smiled a farewell and headed for the door.

"Do send us an invitation to the wedding," Grandmother called to our backs.

Dianne looked like she'd swallowed a frog, something she'd rather do than marry me.

Then I had to stand for a moment holding the car's door handle while I scraped my emotional innards off the ground, like I always have to do after seeing my grandmother. I wish she was up to sneaking off on a cross-country trip with her friends.

Dianne shoved me aside, saying, "I'll drive. You don't know how to navigate Dallas."

Appreciating Dianne's signature empathy, I let her.

VIRGINIA

She was happy to hand the wheel back to me when we reached Arkansas. Being from East Texas, I'm used to pine trees, but Arkansas has pine trees on growth hormones, beautiful during the day, but at night on rural roads, a threatening menace. Dianne snuggled down with her ear buds. I popped mine in and called up music on my phone. I trusted Bach's grinding away to keep me awake.

Dianne woke some time before dawn when I bounced over those little ridges that keep you from wandering onto the shoulder, which I did anyway.

"You must be seeing double." She yawned.

"Nah, I've got one eye closed."

"Pull over. I'm driving."

We changed places after I found a gas station. After loading up with gas and yesterday's donuts, I lay back as far as I could, sure that I wouldn't sleep a wink. I put on Dianne's eye mask and jammed her pillow under my head as I folded myself into a semi-fetal position. The lavender smelled nice, nice enough that I didn't care what it looked like, all satin lilac with embroidered flowers.

By the time I opened my eyes and pulled off the mask, the dark menacing trees were transformed into city concrete in full sun. Maybe we switched planets. Instead of feeling like an ant in my Sonata next to all the F-150 trucks, I was surround by Honda CR-Vs, all silver. Maybe it was a law in these parts.

We were parked outside a Ramada Inn. Dianne was marching into the lobby in full Di-blitz mode.

I washed down a now even staler donut with a warm, flat soda from the previous night. She returned a few minutes later, clutching her arms over her chest to keep warm. Other parts of the country take winter seriously.

"They're not here." She started the car.

"The hotel told you?"

"Not in so many words. I said my *tía* was traveling with a bunch of friends, and my *mami* sent me over to invite them to dinner. I didn't have the room number, but they would have been on the first floor because they were elderly, and one person was in a wheelchair. Nobody like that was registered. So. We go on."

"Want me to drive? Where are we?"

"Harrisonburg, Virginia. And you're not driving without coffee."

Fortunately there was a diner next door, as God intended, though not Miss Leigh's favorite. This journey was starting to feel like spring break trips to Padre Island, jumping in the car after the last class and bearing non-stop down the highway until you hit the beach, except nothing that fun was in our future. That's what they call growing up, right?

I tore into my sandwich as Dianne picked at her salad and said, "There's good odds we're ahead of them now. Let's stay here a bit and watch the road and the Ramada driveway. They'll stop for the night soon, if not here, then somewhere not too far down the road."

We paid the bill, lest we had to resume the chase. We were silently sipping coffee and diet soda (not together) when a badly painted mint green van trundled past. It sported black cling text that read "Flowers by Flora."

We leapt to our feet. Dianne beat me out the door, because I took a second to check my buzzing phone—and another second to read the text. Dianne was starting the engine when I reached the car. I don't think she would have left me behind, but I wasn't going to test that theory.

Luck held with us: The van stopped at a light. We were a couple of cars behind, but the minty fresh green van loomed over all the CR-Vs.

"What now?" Dianne asked.

"We follow. Where's the next Ramada? They'll stop there for sure, since they didn't take this one."

"That would be Strasburg, less than an hour away."

Dusk floated down like a gauzy scarf as we returned to the highway. They'd be harder to follow at night, which was earlier in these parts than back in Texas. We'd have to follow closer, but on the other hand, they couldn't see us as well.

To the right of us, the sky lit up with blue and red flashing lights.

"*Madre de Dios,*" Dianne muttered, her favorite exclamation. She'd grown up telling her mother it was a prayer, which it might be in this case.

I went with a secular version: "Keep going, keep going."

It didn't. The trooper was after our van. After a sharp shriek from the siren, the van slowed and pulled over on the shoulder. Dianne did the same.

Through clenched teeth she said, "When I stop, get out and swish those white boy tail feathers like you've never done before."

I didn't wait that long. I jumped and ran while the tires still crunched gravel. I didn't swish.

"Officer! Is there a problem?" I shouted.

Pro tip: Don't run up to law enforcement officers from behind. It makes them nervous. I help up my hands and apologized, hoping to calm him enough to lower the gun. Oh, and if you can possibly manage it, be white, especially with blonde hair and blue eyes. Being tall helps too.

He didn't shoot me, but he had every chance to. As the gun

lowered—but not much—I asked, "Is my client in trouble? I'm her attorney." I waved at the backseats of the Pacifica, though I couldn't see anyone, what with the tinted windows and dusk glomming down into night.

"Taillight's out." He was a fine specimen of Virginia law enforcement: tall, young, a good choice for Mr. February in the fundraising calendar.

From the driver's seat came a moan.

"You hear that, Miss Leigh?" I raised my voice. "You'll have to take this car back to the dealer. It shouldn't have anything wrong with it, when you just bought it."

The cop's eyes flicked from the cardboard license plate in the back window down the length of the van, taking in the paint job, which couldn't have looked worse if the painter mixed in a bag of sand with the paint and then drove it wet.

"She had a friend paint it," I explained.

He shook his head at the sacrilege.

One of the back windows rolled down, and our sweet little client stuck her head out, her hair still perfectly coifed into a silver crown. Texas hairspray must be made of the same stuff as chewing gum. "Why, JD, aren't you clever to find us! Dianne too. Is something wrong? The girls?"

I glanced back at Dianne, filming with her phone at chest height. She was just a silhouette except when the red and blue lights flashed.

The same lights gave me a stuttering view of the cop scowling at her as he went back to his car with papers from the van's driver. I turned back to Miss Leigh.

"No, they're fine, but worried. You didn't tell them your plans."

"Of course not! I'd never hear the last of it."

The trooper made his way back to us. "Darryl Swann, would you get out of the car?"

The driver moaned again. I studied at him for the first time, wondering if he'd graduated middle school yet. I was disappointed that

I could feel this way before my thirtieth birthday. Soon I'd be yelling at kids to get off the Gregg House lawn.

A voice growled from the very back of the van. "Let me out, Debbie. If my grandson gets out of the car, I get out of the car."

I couldn't see much of her because of the shadows, encroaching night, and her deep walnut skin, but her eyes glittered.

Miss Leigh declared, "I should get out of the car too, because it's my car, and I hired young Darryl to drive it."

A thready voice said, "I'll get out too. Someone help me with my wheelchair."

"Hand me my cane. I'm getting out too," commanded the last occupant.

"Is there a problem?" I asked the cop. "We're twenty minutes from tonight's hotel. I'll follow them all the way there. If we see an auto parts store open, we'll stop. Otherwise, we'll get the light fixed first thing in the morning."

"It's not that," he said, with earnestness. "We got a report to watch for a van full of old ladies, senior citizens, I mean. The van description and the tag don't match, though."

I waved a hand. "Oh, that. Put out by the Brandon family? They never saw the van because it was a present for one of them. I can see how the details might be fuzzy." Keep talking, JD, I told myself. Just like you're speaking in law class. "You heard Miss Leigh. She bought the van, hired a driver, and took her friends on a trip. My firm acts as her assistant—we can show you the paperwork. We can't lose any time because they have an appointment with the Special Counsel in Washington, DC, on Friday morning. Mind if I get my phone out? I can show you."

Miss Leigh stuck her head out the window again. "What? We have an appointment?"

"Yes." When the cop was through reading my phone, I handed it to Miss Leigh. "Courtesy of my grandfather. You left before the arrangements were complete. I can understand wanting to get out on the road—"

The cheering from the van drowned me out. After it faded, I said to the cop. "Do you want to come with us to Strasburg? You can watch each one of them contact their families."

Dianne broke in. "I've already sent a text to our partner. He'll let the families know."

"And then we'll call them ourselves. Seriously, you're welcome to join us at the hotel. It's just off this highway, on Highway 11."

"By Advanced Auto Parts." Dianne abandoned her video for her phone's map feature.

"Which we will visit tonight if it's open, tomorrow morning if it's not. Here's my card, in case we get separated. It's got our main office number too. You can—"

"That's fine," he said, taking my card. "You can go on."

"Are you sure? Because we don't want there to be any doubt."

He walked away, maybe sensing it was the only way to shut me up. We all froze into a tableau, those standing by the road and those sitting in the van. He sat in his car, obviously waiting for us to leave. He won; I eventually had to breathe. The sigh of relief echoed all around me.

Dianne spoke first. "Let's trade places," she said to Darryl. "You ride with JD, and I'll drive the van. Strasburg Ramada, right?"

He confirmed Strasburg and made an attempt to say how he was fine, which she brushed aside.

"*Basta de cuentas.* Every time my cousins or brother got stopped, my mother and I would drive together so one of us could drive their car and the other could drive them home. Paco, he could hardly walk one time. And Julio would sit there and cry. It's just adrenaline. Epinephrine, Johnny would say. You shouldn't drive under the influence of that, any more than alcohol or drugs. Come on, get out."

"My grandson is not leaving me," said Mrs. Langston, loud from the back.

"Come with us," I invited, holding out my arm for Darryl to grab as he, like Cousin Paco, found his legs boneless.

Mrs. Langston shoved her grandson into the passenger seat. She insisted on sitting in the back with the Pepsi and snacks. I wasn't going to argue with her basilisk glare. She wasn't afraid of anybody or anything life could do to her, because it had already been done.

"Sorry to go all white savior on you," I said in their general direction, as I offered water and Pepsi.

Darryl popped the silver top and drank long and deep, ignoring his grandmother's advice that water would be better for him. "You can be purple for all I care. I thought I was gonna die of a busted taillight. Dang! Look at that. It really is out. Must've knocked it loose when I was painting."

All lit up, except for the one taillight, the van eased onto the highway. Before following, I asked Darryl, "Do you feel like telling me about the last few days? Both of you? And if so, do you mind if I call my partner Johnny so I won't have to tell him later?"

When they agreed, I called Johnny, set the phone in the travel cradle, and started the car.

It sounded like Johnny was in a bar. That was impossible.

"Hang on," he said.

I heard the wheelchair's whir. The background noise faded.

"Where are you?" I asked.

"My bedroom, the one downstairs. Chantal threw a party because she thought I was depressed."

"You are, but Chantal's nuts."

"Yes. At least I know how much worse it can be. Dianne texted that you've caught up to the travelers and everybody's fine."

"All true. Riding with me are Mrs. Doria Langston and her grandson Darryl Swann, the driver we kept hearing about. They're going to tell me all about the trip, or as much of it as they can get in before the next Ramada, about twenty minutes away. Mrs. Langston, Darryl, this is my third partner, Dr. Johnny Ly. Now you've met all the Black Orchids."

"Ain't none of you Black," muttered Mrs. Langston from the back seat.

"No, but neither are black orchids. Just very dark purple."

Darryl took the bit and charged. "I don't care, if only somebody else will take over this show. I've been driving my granny around since I got my driver's license, and that's okay, but this—"

His grandmother snorted. "Like you didn't complain every single time."

"Not much, just for show, you know? I take her to the clinic, shopping a bit, out for a bite afterwards. And she pays for my gas. So I said sure when she asked me to drive her and her friends to Washington, 'cause Miss Linda, she's dying and wants to go there for something. I wanted to wait until spring break, but Granny said Miss Linda might not last that long, so I got an excuse from school for a family emergency.

"Then they start playing spies. They don't want anybody to know where they're going. Miss Leigh buys a new van what she's gonna give to her daughter afterwards. I take the batteries out of their phones and get some burners, and Granny says we got to go to Dallas to disguise the van—and I'm supposed to cover it with a bunch of stickers, different ones each day. Mr. Abe-whatsis told me where to make copies of the temporary tag, a new one for each day, just changing one or two numbers."

He paused for breath and another gulp. "I figure that's not really criming, you know, but then turns out they're carrying a—boatload of cash, one of them's got a gun, and one of them's got a box of space cakes, and they're eating them all day long. Even my granny."

"Not all day," muttered his grandmother. "Just one or two."

"They were supposed to be for Miss Linda, with her cancer and all, but everybody had aches and pains."

"Not anymore," Granny testified.

"They all start in on the edibles, saying nothing much is happening, and by today they're giggling all the way and eating everything but their shoes and I have to stop every few hours for more. Snacks, not shoes. And they're talking about breaking into some building in DC, like it'll be the most fun ever! Then Miss Linda says she quit taking her pills on the first day and she's never felt better. And everybody gets out their pill boxes and bottles and throws them all over the van, swearing they're never taking another pill in their lives. Miss Debbie, the official nurse, told them they can't do that, just stop with their medicine. But they just kept giggling. And yeah, you too, Granny."

"That cop sure sobered them up."

I interjected plot points *sotto voce* to keep Johnny on the same page.

"Sobered me up too, and I'm cleaner than a priest on Sunday, totally the party mom, me. Thought there was gonna be Remember Darryl vigils and marches for sure. Gawd, I'm glad you showed up. Was that just luck? Or one of those miracles everybody else gets?"

"I better see you in church next Sunday, Darryl. Don't you go blaspheming when Jesus saved you."

"Oh, I'm not, Granny. I'm not."

I decided not to say that my initials were JD, not JC, but I did interrupt the religious discussion to tell them how Johnny's best guesses led us to this point.

Then Johnny, who hadn't said a word, interjected. "I just sent sent a bare-bones update to all the families. I suggest that everyone call their relatives to confirm their safety."

"And I suggest we do that in the morning, sober," said Mrs. Langston.

"JD, you and Dianne pick up the pills in the car, if that hasn't been done already. Take photos before you pick them up, take another photo if the identifying marks aren't showing. Send them to me. Photos, not pills. But save the pills. I'll send you instructions for the morning. You should be in DC tomorrow, right?"

"Yes, but tonight? We're tapped out too. Besides, we'll see better in the morning."

Johnny insisted, "Tonight's best, JD. Send me the photos right away. And everybody should call a pharmacy, preferably a branch of their local one, and ask for a few days' supply. It's easy to do when you're traveling. And I want to see the list of prescribed drugs for each person."

"Why?" demanded Mrs. Langston. "That's private."

Johnny was quiet. In the background we could hear a booming bass and shrieks of laughter.

"Mrs. Langston, my partners and I are responsible for Mrs. Brandon's safety. We have a right to see hers."

That didn't sound right, but I couldn't research it while driving.

Johnny continued, "By extension, Mrs. Brandon seems to be in charge of this operation, if only because she's paid for most of it. Maybe I'm going overboard, but I don't want any liability to come back to her. Naturally anyone can refuse, but at least they should talk to the pharmacist about whether they can safely stop taking their medicine. My review is just for my own confirmation."

Mrs. Langston snorted. "You're a vet."

"My patients try to get out of taking their medicine too. I'll consult with an MD—without your names, to preserve your privacy." When there was no further objection, he said, "I'll text Dianne the basics and tell her to call when she arrives somewhere." Then in a voice of pure anguish, Johnny cried, "Chantal wants me to come sing with her. I can't—"

The line went dead.

COMMAND CENTRAL

*W*e arrived at the hotel a few minutes behind the van. Miss Leigh was arranging for rooms while Dianne helped Ms. Schliemann into her wheelchair. As Darryl ran inside for a luggage trolley, we lifted out the various bags, while making sure not to disturb any free-floating medication.

I had no idea what Johnny was up to, but ten years' friendship has taught me that he has reasons. And despite the recent damage to his body, his brain still worked. So I took the mag light and a box of snack bags from my car and searched for the discarded medicine. I could have opened a pharmacy with the number of pills these women were taking, so it took me a long time. The van was a big as some college apartments around my university. I gave thanks to any god listening that the state trooper hadn't decided to search the van.

I considered whether buying a bunch of Pacificas, parking them by the university, and renting them to students would be a profitable venture. I gave it up because of the expense of parking passes and the van, which cost more than my grandparents' first house.

By the time I snapped photos, sent them to Johnny, and collected the meds, Dianne and Mrs. Ly had everyone persuaded to call a local pharmacy to beg for a few day's pills—except for Mrs. Schliemann, who was still swearing she was never taking another pill as long as she lived, however short that might be.

"What's it going to do if I don't? Kill me?" she snapped. It was my first look at her, the inspiration for this trip. Small and shrunken, bones the width of toothpicks, I could tell her body was giving up. Her iron-gray hair shone in a beautiful coif, which told me it was a wig. My mother died of cancer when I was in college; her hair always looked great, even in the casket.

I tried to make a tactful suggestion. "It might be painful, going off everything at once. Why don't you at least get a list of what you've been taking?"

"You might think of me," scolded Mrs. Ly, a short chunky woman with snapping black eyes. "You wanted me to come along as your nurse. What kind of trouble am I going to be in if you mess yourself up because you didn't take your medicine?"

Mrs. Schliemann grudgingly made the call while Mrs. Ly turned her gaze on me. I felt like I should show a permission slip.

"How is my grandson?" she asked. "All by himself with a broken foot?"

The last time I saw Mrs. Ly was at our open house, where she held court as a queen accepting tribute from her subjects. She had ruled over Beauchamp and her family for fifty years. Her move to a retirement community seemed a technicality.

I tried to visualize cute little Debbie Schwarz, whose wedding photo still hung over our sofa. She took her nursing degree and her idealism into the Vietnam war and returned with a Vietnamese husband and their first child on the way, thereby stretching her parents' tolerance thin as dental floss. Whatever ravages time had visited on her body, her formidable spirit shone from those eyes as she waited for an answer.

Dianne soothed, "Our friend Chantal is staying with him. You met her at the Christmas party. She sings with us."

"Her?" Mrs. Ly's eyes widened.

Chantal has that effect on people.

I added, "And tonight a bunch of friends came over."

Dianne made a face at me that she tried not to let the others see.

At long last, everyone had contacted a pharmacy. Fortunately, most of them used Walmart. Dianne loaded that crew into the van, and I took Mrs. Ly and Miss Leigh to CVS. They were only too happy to have Johnny look over their medications, both of them confiding their difficulties in getting their doctors to pay attention to them. I sympathized as I shot copies of their lists to Johnny.

I was too tired to wonder about what he was doing with them. We arrived back at the hotel later than the others because my ladies wanted milkshakes before they went to bed. In the rear-view mirror, I saw Mrs. Ly add rum to hers. I knew Miss Leigh was Baptist and wouldn't dream of such a thing. I guess cannabis wasn't mentioned in the church laws.

Miss Leigh whispered, "Maybe just a drop. Such a day it's been!"

Dianne was still in the lobby, talking with Mrs. Ly and Mrs. Schliemann. They said they were going to use the extra time before their appointment to attend a Texas senator's coffee klatch at 10:00 the next day. Then Mrs. Schliemann ended the conversation by shoving a bag of pills into Dianne's hands. "I said I wasn't taking any more. Ever. If you're so curious about them, here they are. Go flush them for all I care."

"Don't do that," whispered Nurse Ly as she pushed the wheelchair.

We called our good nights as Dianne stuffed the pills in her bag. She led me in the opposite direction from the rest of our party. As we passed the bar, almost as big as a postage stamp, she stopped so suddenly that I stepped on her heel. She swung her bag at me in retaliation, but not hard.

It took me a few seconds longer, but she'd needed only the first note to recognize the song, a great classic from our—do I have to say youth? Already? She stood at the entrance, torn between exhaustion—hella eggs, as we said in college—and longing to dance, even in tiny room with tiny tables and a dance floor almost as big as one of the tabletops. Feeling the same pull, I compromised by leading her in progressive cha-cha down the hall. When we couldn't hear the music, I whisper-sang, "Corazon Espinado" until Dianne stopped and pulled out a key card.

She made a face as the door swung open to reveal one bed. "Do you mind? There weren't any other rooms."

I shrugged. "I'd sleep with a pregnant gorilla at this point. Not that I'm making comparisons."

She sniffed. "Thanks." She walked in ahead of me. Three steps to the bed, a wiggle of her hips to shed her leggings, a few wiggles above to scramble out of her bra, a twitch of the bedspread, and she was out.

I shrugged. Since Johnny was so all-fired curious about everybody's medicine, I retrieved Mrs. Schliemann's medicine and set the bottles on the end table with their labels facing out. I took out one pill from each, placed it in front of its bottle, and snapped photos. I sent them to Johnny before heading for the bathroom.

I stood in the shower, with the water as hot as I could stand, my personal therapy for washing the day away. Most of my life I've lived with other people who object to my using all the hot water, so staying in a hotel was a treat. No way I'd use up all their hot water at night. And no one would know if I did.

With skin the shade of boiled lobster, I finally staggered towards bed. Dianne, like she does, had flopped over the whole king-sized thing. I lifted an arm and shoved a leg to make room for myself. She rolled over and fastened herself on me as she muttered something. I wondered how I was going to sleep, with this armful of heaven, scented faintly with her favorite gardenia perfume and totally of Dianne. My next thought was "Huh?" as I blinked awake as sunshine invaded one slit between the drapes.

Dianne stirred beside me, and I wondered for a few seconds exactly how much I had to drink last night. The total was zero, but I felt like I'd been the life of Chantal's party, which takes some doing, because Chantal has been the life of every party she's ever given or attended. It wasn't fair to feel this bad without first feeling good.

I let my hand fall on Dianne's hair, soft and silky, as I said, "*Que pasa, chiquitita?*"

She yawned and wiggled to disentangle herself. I did too, and somehow we ended up facing each other. I stared into those eyes and hoped somebody was going to stop this, because I didn't think it was going to be me. My brain was totally against getting involved with Dianne for a fourth time, but other parts were saying "Fourth time's the charm," and still others didn't care at all.

Dianne's phone clanged. That's another thing old friends do, curse them. As she grabbed the phone, she tossed me aside with a champion-level hip thrust developed from a lifetime of salsa dancing.

I took a second to sigh while she greeted Johnny.

"Oh, he's here," she said, putting the phone on speaker.

"Yeah," I gasped.

"JD, do you still have the medicine? I want you to take one of the capsules to a lab in DC. I've already talked to them and paid for a super-rush job analysis."

"With what?" muttered Dianne, the eternal accountant.

"Why do you think God invented credit cards?" I murmured back. Louder I said, "Sure. We're headed out...er, fifteen minutes ago."

"But why, Johnny?" demanded Dianne. "It's just a capsule, probably probiotics or some other supplement."

Johnny hesitated. "I just—don't you have to be going? I'll tell you later—or not, if I'm just being paranoid."

I began the search for clothes. "I want to hear it anyway, but you're right: we need to get on the road. We have to drop our friends off at the Senate offices. They're going to grade our senator's performance. He'll probably hide in the bathroom."

Dianne added, "And JD will go with them to chase down the senator, and I will go to the lab. Text me the deets. How are things there? Good party?"

The heavy sigh was audible at this distance. "They left by midnight, because we're all grownups now with jobs. Some of us, anyway. Chantal's still asleep. No vet clients yet, and all is blissfully quiet, except for the kittens. I'd rather hear kittens than drunken humans."

"You want to trade for a van full of stoned old ladies?" I retorted.

"We better steal their stash," said Dianne, ever practical.

We didn't have to, because Doria Langston already had. She declared herself the official cannabis edible dispensary and doled out half a chocolate to the arthritis sufferers and one for the cancer patient. Then she put the contraband in my car—thanks a lot—so that they wouldn't take it on government property.

Mrs. Langston scolded her friends, "You want to be clear minded when we meet the senator, don't you? I wouldn't put it past him to call the cops on us."

They agreed that the senator was a jerk—they put it stronger, but I know my grandparents are going to read this. It feels odd to be translating other grandparents for my grandparents.

Senator Smarmy could hardly get a sentence out without my companions accusing him of inaccuracies, contradictions, and hypocrisy. Having introduced myself as their lawyer, I frowned in appropriate spots. Every once in a while I tapped a note into my phone, just for meanness. It was worth it. The senator stuttered every time I did.

"Dang," muttered Darryl. "They really don't give a—um, hoot—about anything, do they? Almost makes me want to get old."

When we met Dianne for lunch, they relived their triumph. Then we repaired to our hotel so the older crowd could take a nap.

Okay, I did too. I don't know if Dianne did; my new roommate was Darryl. He played a game on his laptop with headphones on. Considerate, but I could have fallen asleep in Times Square on New Year's Eve. Or during Chantal's party.

Dianne banged on the door after an hour or so, not nearly long enough, to say Johnny wanted to have a video call with our whole group. We piled into one of the conference rooms and clustered around our phones and tablets and laptops. Dianne brought every device we had.

Johnny greeted us and hoped we were well. He then cut the civilities short to say, "All your families would like to speak with you, some more than others, but they all felt that a text saying 'Am fine. Will call later.' was inadequate." He had to raise his voice over the expressions of disgust. "Not you, Gran. I talked to Dad, and he said 'That's just like her.' I didn't call Aunt Chana. She didn't know anything in the first place."

Mrs. Langston turned to her grandson. "Call your mama, Darryl."

"Ah, Granny," said Darryl, slumping as he reverted to childhood.

She insisted, "At my age, I shouldn't have to ask anyone's permission to go places."

Darryl trudged to an opposite corner of the room to make his call.

I leaned closer to hear Johnny over Darryl's "But Moms."

"Mrs. Schliemann, your children are particularly concerned. I have them connected on meeting software. Dianne, JD, can one of you dial in?"

"All of them?" she asked.

"Yes. Including Shawn Sanders. Buddy is here also. Helping. Miss Leigh, your daughter Claire arrived this morning. If you have time to talk to her now, we'll patch in your daughter Maureen too.

Dianne did things with my tablet, and in a few minutes, we were seeing Vicksburg, Mississippi, and Beauchamp, Texas, from her laptop in a DC hotel. Johnny looked miserable, with Claire on one side and Buddy Hamilton, calling and waving to Mrs. Schliemann, on the other. A kitten, Ginger Tom, sat on top of the recliner and chewed on Johnny's hair. I listened in while I set up the other meeting.

"Mother, what are you doing?" sobbed Maureen, a desiccated version of the free-wheeling Claire.

Miss Leigh's expression was a combination of sweet Southern charm and mule-level stubbornness. "I'm taking a friend to see Washington, DC. I don't know what the fuss is about. I'm still in my right mind."

Claire complained, "You could have told us. Instead you sneak off, and we didn't know what had happened to you. And spending all that money! Not that you don't have it, but you've never spent a nickel you didn't have to."

Miss Leigh sniffed and glared at Dianne, then me. "I'm just fine, as you can see. And it occurred to me that I should enjoy and share the money I have while I can."

"But when are you coming back?" whined Maureen.

"I don't rightly know. I'm thinking I might rather take a plane. Traveling in the car that long makes me stiff, though everyone found your chocolates helpful, Claire. I hope you brought some more."

Claire covered her eyes. "Mother, for heaven's sake. If you'd asked me, I'd have told you how to travel with them."

Miss Leigh turned to her other daughter, who was ready to thunder more condemnation. "Maureen, I wanted this to be a surprise, but I bought you a van, a Pacifica, just like you talked about at Christmas, and Doria's grandson drove us here in it. It's really roomy! Why don't you and Claire come up here and drive it back? I'll have it painted any color you like, though if it was me, I'd choose light blue."

Claire objected, "No, Maureen, you'll want something that stands out."

Her sister snapped, "No, *you* want something that stands out."

"If your mother goes to the trouble and expense of buying you a van—"

With years of practice, Miss Leigh broke up the brewing fight. "Claire, I'll get one for you next year or the next, maybe for your business, since you just bought one a few years ago."

We left the two sisters arguing about the best way to get to DC. I wouldn't have bet a Sonic coupon on their traveling together. I handed Mrs. Schliemann my tablet and followed as she steered her wheelchair to another corner of the room.

After she punched the Join button, the screen showed Shawn Sanders in his home office, with African fabric on the wall behind him as a tapestry. The three Schliemanns were calling from a private office in the dealership, and Buddy was in my office in Gregg House, which made me frown.

"Mother, how could you do this?" began China.

Her mother lifted her chin. "It wasn't easy, but I have good friends."

"We've been so worried," added Sierra.

"Not me," said Buddy. "I knew you could take care of yourself."

"This isn't your affair," Micky snapped.

They complained for longer than I thought necessary until Mrs. Schliemann cut in.

"Okay. Which one of you wants to find me dead?" she demanded.

That shut them up. Daunted, Micky tried to say, "But Buddy—"

"Buddy will glance at my corpse and call one of you. So you need to decide who will deal with my dead body. I've got a list of people to inform, a draft of an obituary, memorial plans, my will, and last instructions, but I cannot take my corpse to the funeral home and clean up afterwards."

"Be sure to call the Justice of the Peace," I added. "Texas law."

Sierra tried. "Mother, there are some things in life that a person just has to do."

"Some things. Not this one. Do you really want me back home for more and more rounds of soggy farewells? How many have we done already? I love you all, but I don't want to spend my last days weeping over my last days. I feel more alive than I've felt for years. I'm having a good time with my friends, one of whom is a nurse and has seen the human body torn up in every way you can imagine. Another spent her career as a secretary for funeral homes, insurance companies, and the city clerk. Between them, they can get my death registered and my remains cremated. You're welcome to come visit me here, if you feel the need—I'll even pay for it—but I have left home for good."

Buddy made an unwise effort on her behalf. "Your mother certainly has the right to decide what makes her happy in this matter."

Even Sierra screamed at him. Micky scarcely paused between tirades, but I was disappointed in China's vitriol. I wouldn't want to wake up to that in the morning. Shawn shook his head and sent his screen black.

Mrs. Schliemann looked up at me. "How do you hang up this thing?"

It was a wise choice.

From the grumpy expressions after they signed off from their nearest and dearest, no one else's meeting went any better. Miss Leigh, backsliding from her financial freedom, rescued the day with a list of free things to do in Washington, DC. Then they fought over what to see and do. Those who had been to DC before wanted to show the newbies all their favorite places. The compromise was to ride the DC Circulator on the Union Station route and make a list of what to see later. I estimated they'd need six weeks to get through all the proposed sites.

DISCOVERIES

The next morning saw us besuited and off to our appointment with destiny. Well, Mrs. Schliemann's destiny. I admired the efficiency of the plan to send us to Tidal Basin. We could see the cherry trees at the same time, and it offered more privacy than the National Mall, where every tree branch has its own tourist.

Washington was a study in contrasts. On the one hand, it had open parks. On the other, it had streets shoved too close together with too many buildings crammed too full of people, some dreamers, some desperate. I don't know the ratio.

I glanced away from the cotton candy–colored (and shaped) trees, just for the pleasure of looking at them again, when I saw two men get out of a taxi—a real taxi, not a rideshare. I've seen taxis in historical photos.

The men were silver-fox distinguished, wearing gray wool suits with sober ties, looking just like my family wanted me to. I suddenly felt that the yellow stripe in my forest green tie was too wild and crazy. My grandfather would think so. He looked a lot like these guys, just as old and distinguished. DC was full of them. Maybe it was a White-Haired White Guy sanctuary?

Or so I told myself until Dianne grabbed my arm. "It's him!"

I was forced to acknowledge to myself that I was standing in the presence of Special Counsel Robert Mueller. Plus an underling whose name I forgot when his boss extended a hand and said, "James Thompson? How's Jimbo? You look just like him."

"Yes. I'm called JD, to keep all the James Thompsons, Attorneys at Law, straight. He was well when I saw him on Tuesday."

"And Arline? Is she still playing the piano? You could count on her at any party to play any piano available for most of the evening."

"She—I don't know. They don't have a piano in their cottage. They're at an assisted living place because of Grandmother forgets things sometimes."

"I'm sorry to hear that. But I bet she could still remember songs from long ago."

I remembered Grandmother playing Christmas carols for hours at our open house. "I hope so, sir. I'll test your theory."

Then I stumbled through introductions, which ended with a piercing gaze from the assistant, who, in a polite and distinguished way, told the young people to get lost. Mrs. Langston protested that after what her grandson had gone through, he ought to be in at the end. Dianne and I agreed and tried to seal the deal by walking away in capitulation. The Special Counsel acquiesced, and Darryl stayed.

As we strolled away down the path, we raised our voices to praise the cherry blossoms and the Tidal Basin lapping at our feet. All the while we kept glancing over our shoulders.

Mr. Mueller guided Mrs. Schliemann's wheelchair away in the opposite direction. The rest of the group returned to the van and opened the doors so that some could sit down. Mrs. Ly unfolded her cane into a stool. The underling spoke with them, or at least to them.

"Do you think that will be us in fifty years?" asked Dianne with a last glance at the women. "Still together, going off on adventures?"

"Probably," I said. "I'll be a special counsel, and Johnny will discover all kinds of stuff I should know. I hope he gets out of the wheelchair and stays out. You'll find all kinds of fraud in the financial records, and we'll all be on the news every night. I imagine our families will be used to it by then."

Actually, old age with Dianne, Johnny, and Chantal seemed more believable than the currently mythical spouses we were supposed to acquire. Dianne's frown told me she was thinking the same thing.

We kept walking, making a game of trying to spot the security forces that had to be close by. Half a mile away, we reached the point of wondering what we'd do if we met the Special Counsel and Mrs. Schliemann when we saw them turn around on the far side of the basin. We did the same, picking up our pace.

Farewells were graceful and quick, with me promising to deliver greetings to my grandparents and everyone else expressing gratitude.

Afterwards a hush hung over our group, normally chatty with or without herbal assistance. It was like an especially ineffable church service—I hear those exist for some people. We stood in the cogs and gears of democracy, working with all those checks and balances, as we spoke with our employees, the public servants paid for by our taxes. I'm from a cynical generation; I needed a shot of the idealistic vision just as much as my older companions did.

After a quick lunch that I don't remember, we went back to the Basin and rented paddleboats for an hour. I paddled for Mrs. Schliemann, Mrs. Ly, and Mrs. Langston, and Darryl and Dianne paddled in another boat with the rest of the passengers. Conversation was sparse, except for variations on "You are going to tell us what he said, right, Linda?" The answer was always, "He said I mustn't ever tell a soul, and I'm not."

Up close, the individual cherry blooms were five- or ten-petaled flowers bursting out of a nest of tiny leaves on pink-tinged branches. More restrained flowers have filament-like stamens tipped with golden pollen, but cherry blossoms have a cluster, making the petals, shades of white through deep pink, look polka-dotted, as though the short-lived blossom was determined to spread itself as far and wide as possible.

"This here's worth the whole trip," said Mrs. Langston from her seat in the back. "I've got a pear tree in my yard, and I purely love it in spring when it's in bloom. The fruit's little and sour. My son always wants to chop it down. I tell him I want it for the shade, because he wouldn't understand putting up with it all year for three weeks of blossoms.

"I'm glad I got to see them. They weren't in bloom the last time I was here," said Mrs. Schliemann, her voice full. "Cherry blossoms are a symbol of life, beautiful and fleeting."

It seemed to be the moment to pull out cameras and phones for photos. I blinked in surprise that people still had cameras, but after all, these particular people were over seventy.

"You'd think something so beautiful would smell better," said Mrs. Langston, breaking the awe.

"It's bittersweet," scolded Mrs. Schliemann. "Like life."

"Go all poetic if you want to, Linda. If I smelled that in my refrigerator, I'd clean it on the spot."

"I've frequently felt that way about life," said Mrs. Ly from the front seat.

I was taking my own photos when my phone cheeped at me with a text. Johnny wanted Dianne and me to see whether anyone else had capsules like the one Dianne took to the lab. I sighed at the thought of going back to work, but it made Dianne's subsequent text easier to bear. They were headed back to the dock because our hour on the boats was almost up. I asked Johnny's question as I handed my phone with the pill's photo visible to Mrs. Ly, who passed it around the boat. Mrs. Schliemann couldn't remember, and the others didn't think it was theirs either.

I made a big turn into the center of the basin to give us a panoramic view of the fluffy pink shoreline. I wanted to burn the sight into my mind forever.

Johnny's text said he had to talk to Mrs. Schliemann alone. Highly confidential. I'd no sooner finished reading it than Dianne pinged me to say we should meet in her room. It was closer to Mrs. Schliemann's room.

This time we used video conferencing on Dianne's laptop. Johnny looked like he was in a closet with a backdrop of flowered dresses.

He was. He'd locked his bedroom door and backed his wheelchair into the closet, where his grandmother kept a few clothes. It was quieter.

"I don't want anyone listening at the door. The refrigerator is on the other side of the wall, and the pantry's next to it; I don't think anyone can hear from the kitchen."

Mrs. Schliemann gasped with astonishment. "What on earth could you have to say to me that needs to be that secret?"

"I'm sorry to say that someone is trying to kill you."

"Kill me? I'm dying. What on earth do you mean?"

"I mean that you took one capsule every day that was laced with poison, something you'd use in the garden. I just received the report from the lab."

Dianne reached out and held the older woman's hand.

Mrs. Schliemann was still in shock. "But why?"

"I don't know yet. I just know what was done. Quitting your medications was the best thing you could do."

"No wonder I felt better!"

"No wonder. Who profits from your death, and how much?"

She laughed, a sour note. "I'm not Leigh Brandon, oil magnate widow. Jack built the car dealership up, and the kids are running it now. There's the house, but it was built in the 70s. Shawn was the only one who wanted it. He gets an additional stipend, and the others will split what's left, which, besides the dealership, might add up to a really nice vacation, new car, or college fund, nothing to kill over."

"You'd be amazed. What about timing? Does anyone need their

share now? What about Buddy?" Johnny grimaced. "He comes over every day to make sure I'm okay. Claire's here too."

I tried not to grin. Just the recipe for driving Johnny into a closet to take a phone call.

Mrs. Schliemann shook her head. "No. When I started dating after Jack died—goodness, it's been twelve years now—I promised the kids I wouldn't give their inheritance to another man. That's one reason I didn't marry again. Buddy is ten years older than me. We didn't think he'd be the survivor, but early this year I paid his way into a retirement home for him to have somewhere to go after I die while he waits for a place in a VA facility. There's no telling how long that will take. I never intended to do any more for him. He knew it and my kids knew it. He wasn't after my money. Now Sylvan, the one before him, he was out to get his hands on whatever he could. I threw his ass out five years ago."

"Who's visited you since you received your prognosis?"

"The kids, my friends—all the women here, of course. The other Promisers. People from the church. I didn't tell too many people, though I imagine it's spread all over town anyway. They can weep over me, or pretend to, at my funeral. I hadn't gotten around to calling hospice. How much training do you need to die?"

"Then I suggest you don't share this issue with your children or Buddy. Invite them to another digital meeting this evening at 7:00 your time, because you have something you want to say to them all. I'll host the meeting here. If you think of anyone else who's been in your house, let me know before then. And since we've been acting for you, please sign a statement giving Black Orchid Enterprises and their representatives permission to do so."

With best wishes for her continued health, which seemed out of line, he signed off.

Emotions bubbling on a low boil, she twisted around to look at me. "I want you to make me a new will."

"I have will forms on my laptop," said Dianne, retrieving it and searching. "Contracts too. Can you adapt Miss Leigh's contract to this situation, JD?"

I nodded as I took the laptop from her. "Would you like us to send the invitations for tonight? Dianne could do that from your phone."

"I don't know what the point is, but that young man seems to have something in mind," said Mrs. Schliemann.

That's always true about Johnny.

She handed her phone to Dianne as she recited the names of her visitors. After I gave her the go ahead, she recited the terms of her new will. "I leave $10 to each of my four children, my sister, Buddy, and anybody else who thinks they have a claim on me. Oh hell, my brothers too. And better include Jack's brother and sister, not that I've seen them since he died, but best to be safe. Now where can I leave my estate where it will annoy people the most?"

"Depending on your family, a political party might be annoying enough," said Dianne, leaning over my shoulder as I typed.

"But her friends are in the same party," I said. "We have to annoy them too. The Boy Scouts, Young Mothers, and Friends of Animals also meet at our house. The Friends want to build space for more animals and make Beauchamp a no-kill city. Is that annoying enough?"

"All three are fine. Leave out the Promisers, just in case, though I really don't think my friends would go on a trip with me and poison me at the same time. Print it out and I'll sign it."

Dianne's little portable printer took forever to spew out the will and the contract. Dianne and I witnessed the will. When the last signature was added, Mrs. Schliemann crumpled, now looking like a dying woman. "I think—if it's not too much trouble—I'd like to lie down for a while before the meeting. I—what could this person be thinking? I'm dying. If they need money now, I could give them thousands of dollars as a tax-free gift. Who hates me enough to kill me? That's all it could be. My parents, sure, for marrying Benny Sanders and having his baby, but they've been dead for a decade. My brothers, whom I haven't seen in years. Benny's mother was kind and helpful, but the rest of the Sanders family—they weren't best pleased when I married Benny, but they can't say they didn't get to see Shawn, and I paid Shawn's way, from his $7 scouting fees to his college tuition each year. Shawn doesn't hate me, I'm sure—I've tried to be fair to everyone all my life, to do the right thing. Why does someone want to take away the few days I have left?"

I murmured disjointed nothings as I wheeled her back to her room, where Mrs. Langston was waiting to ease her friend into bed. Tears streaked down her cheeks in shining lines, but Mrs. Langston didn't ask the reason. She just pulled a sheet up and murmured more standard comfort—and another half of a chocolate.

By then it was time to take Darryl to the train station. With Dianne and me on hand to get the travelers home, he could get back for the last week of classes before spring break. I felt honored that his grandmother trusted me to drive him when she'd scarcely let him out of her sight since I met them. She explained that her friend was in a bad way and might need her, and I seemed to be trustworthy.

She handed Darryl a check from Mrs. Schliemann.

"Miss Leigh already paid me for driving you guys," Darryl objected.

"Darryl, one lesson you need to learn is that when someone wants to give you money, you say thank you. I'll tell her for you, but you send her something too, even a text. And you call me from every stop along the way, you hear?"

"I could send you a text."

"No, you will not. If it's the middle of the night, I'll have the ringer off, but I want to wake up to a bunch of voicemails from you. You understand?"

Dianne was going to go with us, but her phone gurgled as we headed to the car. She swore at it and said to me, "Johnny." We sighed in unison, and she turned back to the hotel. She looked at Darryl over her shoulder. "Maybe you already have a job."

"If I did, would I be driving my granny anywhere—and now I can say anywhere—she wants to go?"

"Seeing how…resourceful…you are, would you like an internship with Black Orchid Enterprises? We need somebody with initiative."

That's one way to describe orchestrating this trip on the down-low, fixing phones and car to be untraceable, and disguising the car.

Darryl's face glowed. "Would I? Man, I'd clean kennels!"

"Good. Because you will. You'll be in training as a receptionist, vet tech, tax preparer, and whatever JD can use you for."

"Social media maven," I said with relish.

She gave me the evil eye and went on. "We can't pay much, but you could have one of the apartments out back, if you help us get it fixed up. Johnny wants someone sleeping by the cat shelter. And you can eat with us. Johnny cooks vegetarian, but JD and I will share our secret meat stashes."

"Wow. Just wow. When do I start?"

"Let's say the week after spring break. It's not that far away."

All Darryl said on the way to the train station was, "Wow." Many times.

FINAL MEETING

When we signed in to the digital meeting room, Dianne and I looked at each other and said in unison, "Chantal."

She'd outdone herself. Behind Johnny's gold recliner stood two of the life-sized cutouts we had made to promote MultiABBA. There was me, trying for a manly expression while wearing a yellow satin suit. The other was Dianne in her yellow bandage dress, with her legs spread wide, one finger pointing skyward, in a nod to that 70s vibe.

Mrs. Langston pursed her lips at Dianne. "Does your mother allow you to wear such outfits?"

"I didn't ask her," retorted Dianne, tossing her hair. "It's a stage costume."

"Even worse. The audience can see straight to Florida."

"Not if you wear matching Lycra shorts," insisted Dianne.

Mrs. Langston and her friends squinted at the screen as Chantal, wearing a similar dress, took her seat next to Johnny.

I was sure there had been a discussion about Johnny wearing his satin suit, but he'd emerged victorious. He wore a yellow cotton dress shirt with a red blanket covering his elevated legs—a good thing, because he'd worn nothing but running shorts since the accident.

Johnny said, "You all agreed to come here and listen to what might be Linda Schliemann's last words to you. Every one of you visited Mrs. Schliemann after her terminal diagnosis, most of you from a wish to express your love and support for her. I'm turning the meeting over to her for her initial statement."

Mrs. Schliemann cleared her throat. "I have indeed appreciated the love and support from my friends and family. Imagine my surprise to find that at least one of you tried to kill me, to rob me of my last few precious days on this earth." She held up a hand to quiet the exclamations in Beauchamp and in the same room with her. "I have taken steps to stop the process, and I have changed my will, which may interest some of you."

She read the document I drew up for her.

"Mother! That's not fair!" exclaimed China, sounding like the youngest child that she was.

"It doesn't make any sense to punish us all for what one person did," argued Micky.

Shawn Sanders shook his head. "Come on, it's classic Mother. Don't you remember that time we went to Six Flags Amusement Park and China threw a tantrum? Mother made us all leave. That's how she is."

Judging from the looks directed at China, her siblings remembered the occasion well.

"And neither she nor any of you ever pulled that stunt again, did you?" Mrs. Schliemann snapped. "I'd like to point out that I don't know who or how many of you did this to me. Perhaps Dr. Ly has some thoughts."

Dianne returned the presenter's mode to Johnny, who leaned back in his recliner and steepled his fingers.

"Thank you, Mrs. Schliemann. I do have some thoughts. For those of you wondering, the attempt on your mother's life consisted of introducing a new medicine that was actually capsules of powdered sugar laced with poison. It must have been easy to do, because her medical regime had just changed to palliative care. Also, her attitude changed from intense involvement with her treatment to indifference, even avoidance.

"Fortunately, her friends intervened to help her with a quixotic quest, during which she decided to forgo all her medications in favor of alternative pain treatment."

"Good, isn't he?" said Mrs. Ly with pride.

"You'd think she'd be grateful enough to those good friends to tell them what the Special Counsel told her," grumbled Mrs. Langston.

"You know she promised him she wouldn't," scolded Miss Leigh.

Mrs. Langston suggested, "Maybe she could leave us a note, to be opened later."

"Hush," commanded Mrs. Schliemann in her teacher's voice.

They did.

Johnny continued, "I first wondered about Mrs. Schliemann's health when I heard that she went into a wheelchair the same week her treatment stopped. I don't say such a rapid decline is unheard of, but my practice is to make note and watch for confirming signs.

I glanced at Dianne. While we're adults who do not roll our eyes, I could tell she was remembering Johnny confronting us about something and reciting a list of indications that led him to his conclusions.

He continued, "Suffice to say, just after we established contact with our travelers, I asked them to provide a list of their medications, with the idea that perhaps she was reacting negatively to one or another. I asked a pharmacist and a medical doctor review the lists I received. Most of the travelers have resumed most of their medications, some intending to have discussions with their physicians when they return. But one capsule—perhaps you'd like to explain its packaging, Chantal."

Chantal leaned forward, delighted to have a speaking role. She wiggled her shoulders, and the men on camera dropped their jaws. I clenched mine tighter so as not to be a pig. Besides, I'm used to Chantal.

"Today it's easier than ever to fake documents. The poisoned capsule came from one of Mrs. Schliemann's bottles—"

"Established by an independent laboratory," Johnny interjected.

"Yes. It was a pharmacy bottle, with what looked like a pharmacy label, good enough to fool most people but not a graphic design professional." She leaned back and wiggled again to make it clear whom she was talking about. I heard a sigh from the lower voices in the room.

"She's wearing little yellow panties," Mrs. Langston explained to Miss Leigh, who shook her head.

"Remember those miniskirts we wore?" she whispered. "Did we look like that?"

"If I ever looked like that—well, I wish I'd known, that's all. I'd be queen of New York."

Chantal continued, "Even from a photo, I could see it was a forged label. Some characters were uneven, like threes altered to eights or sevens to ones—like the travelers did with their temporary tags, changing them enough that they wouldn't show in any search." As a murmur of disapproval welled around her, Chantal suddenly looked like a ten-year-old caught telling what she wasn't supposed to tell.

The ladies in our room groaned. I foresaw pointed conversations for them, a depressing thought, to think that at the end of your life you'll be having teenager-type conversations, but with you as teenager and your middle-aged children as parents. Maybe Dianne's right: Just don't have kids.

Johnny picked up the story as Chantal cringed in her chair. "Mrs. Schliemann's medications had a cuckoo capsule, a deadly imposter. My colleague—" He nodded at Chantal. "—says that the print technology is within the reach of the general populace—"

"Heck, you could pay someone five bucks on fiverr.com to do it for you, and who would ever look?" Chantal interrupted.

"Quite. And you can buy capsules to mix your own supplements. Not a difficult process, but why would anyone do so? Mrs. Schliemann's large family and circle of friends made an unacceptably large group of suspects, none with an obvious motive. Mrs. Schliemann could have given a large tax-free gift to any loved one needing it—a more certain and faster process than waiting on a lengthy probate of the will.

"I came to the conclusion that the motive was not monetary. I tentatively absolved Mrs. Schliemann's traveling companions. Most people want gruesome deaths to happen a long way away. Her family is represented only by her children, and while I'm sure they have their resentments and secrets, like any other family, none seemed to warrant murdering Mrs. Schliemann. The most outwardly troubled person was her eldest son Shawn—"

He lurched forward in a yellow chair. "You think you're pinning this on me?"

"But the more open the resentment, the less likely it would culminate in murder. From my conversations with Mr. Sanders, he doesn't blame his mother for the war in which his father died."

"But I do blame you for marrying him. Why did you do it?" demanded Shawn into one of the cameras.

Mrs. Schliemann rasped out a sigh. "Because he wanted it so much, and not just so the draft board would let him stay with a wife and child, which they didn't do anyway. Benny wanted a child so badly. Now, looking at you, more real to me than Benny has been for fifty years, I wonder how we could have done such a thing to you, but then, you were an unknown, just a fantasy." She made a gesture. "I've saved his letters, his war diaries, for you. You didn't want them when you were younger, but I didn't want to throw them away."

"I don't remember you saying anything about them!"

"It's been many years now. We've both forgotten things." His mother leaned her head on her hand.

Johnny picked up the thread. "I wasn't inclined to suspect Mr. Sanders even before considering that he was a staunch member of recovery groups and his mosque. Mr. Sanders's sobriety depends on his following the dictates of these groups. Mrs. Schliemann's other children have shouldered her care during treatment, taking her to chemo appointments and then caring for her at home, but they don't seem to be at the end of their ropes. They would be relieved of many duties if Mrs. Schliemann entered hospice care. At first glance, I was inclined to dismiss all her children as suspects, although they had more access to their mother's medications than a casual visitor."

The doorbell rang, making his audience jump. Johnny just raised an eyebrow, and Chantal rose to answer the front door. We couldn't see that far, but when Chantal returned, she was leading Officer Alejandro Quintanilla-Villanueva to a seat in the second row of chairs. He was doing his best to maintain a professional, blank face, but he couldn't help grinning at Johnny, who in turn gave his painful eighth-of-an-inch acknowledgement. Only twenty-two years old, Officer Al recently graduated from police academy and joined the Beauchamp police force. You could tell he was living his life's dream when he cautioned you about your loud party and wrote you a warning for speeding, not from a place of power but service, keeping his commu-nity safe. He could scarcely contain his excitement over his first big case.

On my side, everyone crowded closer to their shared screens.

Johnny waited for Chantal to return to her chair. She bristled with excitement while making obvious efforts to remain still and calm. She's good at neither, but I appreciated the effort.

Johnny continued his story. "Only one person expressed no concern at all over the travelers. On the surface, this attitude seemed reasonable. Mrs. Schliemann and her friends are adults who can decide for themselves what they would like to do. Indeed, though they felt it necessary to conceal their flight, they made careful plans, including buying a comfortable van, hiring a driver, and bringing a nurse and a records professional."

"Records professional," said Mrs. Langston with satisfaction. "That's nicer than what they usually called me."

"I began looking at Mr. Hamilton. He made that easy by spending a good part of his days here, offering 'help' during this difficult time. I noticed, though, that he never did anything. He offered many suggestions to my friend in her culinary and personal care efforts, but the one place I really needed help, the vet clinic, he refused to enter at all, on the grounds he had no training." Johnny took a sip of water. "Very little training is required to hold small animals still during examinations or to keep surfaces and litter boxes clean."

"But way too much effort for Prince Buddy," muttered Mrs. Schliemann. "This sounds just like him."

Her friends exchanged looks.

"Indeed, the care of Mrs. Schliemann during her treatment fell to her children, despite her living with a partner. With Mrs. Schliemann's permission, I sent Chantal and Mrs. Brandon's daughter Claire to the Schliemann house today to pack more clothes for Mrs. Schliemann. I hoped they would have the chance to search for evidence. Mr. Hamilton insisted on going along and actively prevented them from searching. I called this meeting tonight to give the police time to search the property, which appears to have been fruitful. Yet despite all these indications, I could see no motive."

Chantal turned one of the screens to show Officer Al standing behind the sofa. He ducked his head in embarrassment as all eyes turned toward him.

Mrs. Schliemann scooted forward in her wheelchair until the screen was inches away from her face. "I'll tell you the motive. He didn't want to see me suffer and die because it was too hard on him. He didn't care about me—he knew I wanted every breath I had left. I told him so when he said he'd get me euthanasia drugs if I wanted to check out early. His wife died of cancer—maybe you should look into *her* death."

Her eldest son growled, "My brother and sisters asked me to look into him when you started dating him. He left his wife months before she died. We actually thought that was a good thing."

Mrs. Schliemann acted like she hadn't heard. "When my dog was sick, he kept telling me to have her put down, and I kept telling him I would when she wasn't enjoying life. Oh, God. Did you poison her? Did you? I'll never forgive you, never!"

"Linda. Linda." Mrs. Langston pulled her friend back and turned her wheelchair away from the screen.

Mrs. Schliemann disappeared in her friends' hugs. On the other side, her children hogged the screen as they shouted, "Mother! Mother, are you all right?"

"Can you talk to them?" asked Mrs. Langston. "We can tell them we'll call back later."

Mrs. Schliemann shook her head and spun her chair to face the cameras.

Buddy was saying, "Of course I didn't kill your dog. I know how you loved her."

"You're lying scum, but I'm going to believe you so I don't die of grief. But you get out of my house tonight. I don't care where you go, but tonight you leave. Shawn, you can move in whenever you like. If...if I come back, maybe you'll let me stay in your house."

Johnny broke in. "Mrs. Schliemann, you called me after hours when your dog reached her limit. I spoke with your vet in Elrod before coming to your house, and I saw no signs of poison, no indication of anything beyond your vet's diagnosis." He nodded to the back of the room. "Buddy is definitely leaving tonight. He's now in the custody of Officer Quintanilla-Villanueva."

I thought I saw the young policeman's hands shake as he cuffed his prisoner.

"I don't want..." Mrs. Schliemann bit her lip. "Oh, hell, yes I do. Fry the bastard for all I care. Children—" She held up her new will and tore it across four times. "JD, does that make my previous will in effect?"

"Yes, and I'll make notes to that effect," I said, putting my arms around Dianne, who was shaking.

"Now everything's back like it was, split between the four of you as we discussed, with bequests to the church and Shawn's mosque."

They all looked shocked.

"Really, Mama? The mosque?" squeaked Shawn. Normally he's a bass-baritone, like me.

"I'd give to the Pastafarians if they'd done as much for you. Now if you all don't mind, I'm going to bed. I'll be happy to talk to you tomorrow."

"You're still not coming back home?" asked Sierra, forlorn.

"I don't know, dearest. I feel like I've said my goodbyes, and I don't know how much time I have left. But all of you children are welcome to visit me here. I want to see the cherry blossoms in full bloom. This is only the beginning of their season. If I make it that far, then I'll see. DC is a lovely place." Her face turned to stone as she watched Officer Al march his prisoner out the door.

Johnny sank far back into his recliner and bowed his head. Chantal and Dianne bid farewells and started everybody else doing the same. In a minute, all the screens went dark.

Mrs. Schliemann slumped in her chair and covered her face. "Why was it so wrong to want somebody's hand to hold when I die?"

"You're not wrong. He is," said Mrs. Langston. "I never did like him, Linda."

"You have to understand about a man that age—" began Miss Leigh. Loud raspberries from her friends covered her last words.

"No, we don't, Leigh," said Mrs. Ly.

"Well, there's not many choices at our age," said Mrs. Schliemann.

"There's the perfectly fine choice of being done with the old coots," said Mrs. Langston. "My husband wasn't perfect—no one is—but he was sure better than what else is out there. And you might consider, Linda, that if you wouldn't insist on a man, you have any number of friends and your children too who'd be glad to hold your hand."

Two friends reached for a hand, and the other patted her shoulder.

Dianne slung her devices into her bag. She shoved right into me, pushing me towards the door with her as she muttered, "That better not be us someday."

I looked back at our clients, but they just waved and called good night as they clustered around Mrs. Schliemann, slumped low in her chair.

OLD FRIENDS

$\mathcal{D}$ianne steered me toward the deserted hotel bar, not the cool place to go on Friday night. The bartender, previously bored, looked annoyed with his prospective customers. But after a few smiles at him, Dianne got access to the music system and programmed the music she wanted. I'm sure it helped that we didn't ask him for drinks.

With a Latin beat pulsing the room, she swept me onto the postage-stamp-sized dance floor for a furious salsa, followed by a cha-cha, just as relentless. We weren't trading lingering looks; she was just losing herself in movement and music. There's a song that talks about how anybody could be the guy, but I didn't quote it, she having told me that ABBA is not the Bible. I doubled her spins and pulled out the most complicated moves I knew—she requires her serious boyfriends to learn to dance, at least the Latin dances, so they can go with her to *quinceañeras*, weddings, and other family occasions. (Learning Spanish is the other requirement, in case you'd like to get prepared.) Besides, she just likes to dance, whether patterned or freestyle wiggling. I've seen her do the Chicken Dance at a Texas wedding, but sadly there's no video.

I had her in a deep dip with her leg around my waist when my phone buzzed in my pocket. Both of us jumped. I grabbed as she fell, her eyes full of terror, and it threw me off balance. Dianne is not overweight—I've been telling her that for ten years—but she has enough pounds on her to drag me down. Hoping for superpowers, I yanked myself back and her up, sliding towards a table at the same time, thankfully close by. Fortunately no one was sitting there.

Dianne flopped like a flounder backwards over a two-foot diameter table, and I'm hanging onto her, the table, and a nearby chair.

"Get a room, kids," called the bartender, bored.

"Not sure I can get there," muttered Dianne, as she squirmed to right herself.

I pulled her from the table into the nearest chair and called to the bartender, "Bring us doubles—what do you want, Dianne?"

The Queen of the One-Glass-of-Chardonnay Club said, "Bourbon. On the rocks. JD, answer the phone, since it almost killed us."

When Dianne's music stopped, I could hear the ring as well as feel the buzz as some determined person called again. I signaled to the bartender to bring me a bourbon too as I fumbled my phone out.

It was Chantal, of course, on video. She was sitting on the arm of Johnny's chair. He looked like something stuffed. I've seen more lifelike figures in the taxidermy museum.

"Okay, you guys. 'The Way Old Friends Do,' key of Dianne's choice, in one-two—"

"Huh?" Alto and baritone sounds came from Dianne and me.

"I mean it! Now! Three-four! Dianne, we need you on melody."

Out of habit, Dianne croaked out the first line.

"Pick one key, Dianne. How can we harmonize with that? Johnny, you're flat. JD, you're a mess."

"I'm not warmed up," Dianne protested. She sipped her drink and made a face. The bourbon had a nice smokey smell.

"How can I be flat if we don't have a key?" asked Johnny.

"Come on, you guys," protested Chantal.

"Oh, okay. Here's my note." Dianne hummed, and we all found our places.

After four wind-tunnel breaths, we started again, singing about friends in silence, finding comfort.

Chantal hollered, "Louder, Dianne. More bass, JD."

"We're in public," Dianne said before belting out the next line.

"So put out a hat," Chantal advised. "We can use the money."

I bolstered Dianne's melody line and moved closer. I propped the phone against my glass to make it easier for both of us to sing into its mic. I wouldn't be drinking immediately. Dianne slowed the last few beats to end the song, but Chantal cranked it up again.

On the third time, between verses, I said, "How many times, Chantal?"

"Until it doesn't sound like a dirge or caterwauling cats. Come on, guys, this is an easy one."

Dianne and I locked gazes and sang our hearts out—softly, though the bartender didn't seem to care. He turned up the sports channel.

After twice more, Chantal let Dianne take us out. Johnny's face had gained color.

"Everybody okay?" asked Dianne. "Johnny?"

He sighed deep down to the basement. "There aren't any happy endings in this work."

Crinkling her brow, Dianne said, "But the truth's got to be better than believing a lie, isn't it? And the truth is, she has many people who love her and would help her in her last days." She shot a sideways glance at me.

"We should all be so fortunate," I proclaimed in wide-eyed innocence.

Blushing, as though she recalled her previous hope that we would not end up like these ladies, Dianne put her arms around my waist and squeezed. "I hope we are."

I answered with another squeeze.

"Life makes no sense," declared Chantal. "You just gotta sing. Let's try—"

"We did sing," said Dianne. "We're tired."

"You're okay, Johnny?" I asked.

He turned up the ends of his lips. "I can live with it."

"Call us tomorrow when you get up," Chantal instructed. "We'll sing until we're all human again. And Johnny's going to teach me to make lasagna. Vegetarian, but I can cure that."

We promised. After I tapped the call off, we pushed our chairs away from each other and addressed ourselves to our drinks, now with water instead of ice.

"That was lovely," said a gravelly voice behind us. "Your dancing too."

Mrs. Ly stood behind us. She came from a table around the other side of the bar.

"I wanted to tell you our plans," she said. "Tomorrow we'll go look at some temporary suites—this town's full of them, and Linda's going to rent one for three months in Doria's name so that we can stay on. She's promised to arrange for hospice services on Monday. Leigh's hoping her family will come get the van, but if not, Darryl can get it on spring break, and she'll probably go back whenever the van leaves."

"We'll get home to Johnny as fast as we can," said Dianne.

His grandmother twisted her lips in a fleeting smile. "I think Johnny is doing just fine. He's a lucky young man to have such good friends."

"We think we're the lucky ones," Dianne said.

I put an arm around Dianne's shoulder. "We can leave tomorrow. I just want to stop long enough to buy my grandmother a practice keyboard and take it to her. She still knows her music, like the Special Counsel said, and she shouldn't be without it."

Dianne answered with an arm around my waist. We were getting proficient at this language.

After a brief smile at each of us and no remarks at all about marriage, Mrs. Ly clumped away.

As we walked down the hall to our rooms, Dianne said, "You didn't drop me."

"Never," I answered.

If you enjoyed Birth of the Black Orchids, please leave a review at your favorite online bookstore or venue. A review ranks close to a book sale as the best present you can give an author. For gifts and news of the next publications, be sure to sign up for the occasional newsletter at https://dimond.me.

ACKNOWLEDGMENTS

Even if I typed just first names in a 6 pt font, the list would be as long as another story, and I'd be sure to leave out people. So I'll just say thanks to my family (including the cats), my friends, and my teachers for traveling the road with me to this point. What a long, strange journey it's been!

ABOUT THE AUTHOR

An emerging author of mystery and science fiction who lives in Texas, M. R. Dimond served stints in professional orchestras, law firms, cat rescue, bookkeeping, and technical communication before returning to a childhood dream of writing fiction, which has turned out to be about musicians, lawyers, veterinarians, accountants, and cats. Previous works include short stories in *Strange Horizons*; *Dancing USA*; *Infinite Space, Infinite God*; and most recently in *Cat Tails: War Zone* and *Dreaming the Goddess*.

facebook.com/madeleine.dimond
twitter.com/MRDimondAuthor
instagram.com/MRDimondAuthor

ALSO BY M. R. DIMOND

"**Blessed**" in *Dreaming the Goddess*, featuring Rosemary Edghill, edited by Karen Dales. *Delve into the Dream.*

"**Nine Lives Through Time**" in *Cat Tails: War Zone*, edited by Dana Bell and Rebecca McFarland Kyle. Twenty-five stories from Ancient Egypt to the far-flung future, about some amazing cats who have served as compatriots during war times.

CPSIA information can be obtained
at www.ICGtesting.com
Printed in the USA
BVHW070200281221
625039BV00005B/336